My sense is--most people today don't want to be challenged to think. If that describes you, don't read this book! But if you enjoy being confronted with new perspectives, and truly desire to know the truth--this book is for you.

Jim Reimann, Editor of the #1
Best-Selling Updated Editions of
My Utmost for His Highest
and *Streams in the Desert*

Several recent books have described the modern day lies that are the foundations for today's beliefs and behavior. Lies about truth, God and faith. But Parker Hudson puts flesh and blood on these lies. His stories explore the inevitable results of living outside of truth. While Parker makes it clear that the stories and the dialogues are fiction, they grip the reader because we already know all the characters: they are our family, friends, neighbors and colleagues. This well written fiction is more real than reality.

Michael Youssef, Ph.D., Author of
Divine Discontent

Parker Hudson's book TEN LIES AND TEN TRUTHS is must reading. Brilliant and insightful, it teaches using contemporary parables that are fun to read and convicting. Read it today and give it to your friends.

Dr. Ted Baehr, Publisher of
Movieguide(r)

D1016670

For Tiffany and John
May God bless you with
His grace and truth

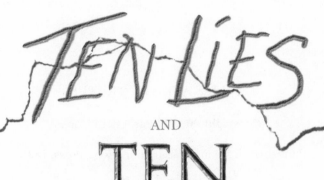

AND

TEN
TRUTHS

Parker Hudson

Edge Press | Atlanta, Georgia

TEN LIES AND TEN TRUTHS

Copyright 2005 F. Parker Hudson

Published in Atlanta, Georgia by Edge Press, LLC

Edited by Suzan Robertson

Cover design by Marshall Hudson

Printed in the United States of America

International Standard Book Number 13: 978-0-9666614-2-2

International Standard Book Number 10: 0-9666614-2-7

Library of Congress Control Number: 2005926003

For information:

www.tenliesandtentruths.com

www.edgepress.net

FOR OUR GRANDCHILDREN

AND THEIR GRANDCHILDREN

That they may love, seek and defend the truth

FOREWORD

These stories have been three years in the writing and refining, and it is our hope that they will linger in the reading.

We hope that you are touched by each of the stories, and that they cause you to ask among your family, friends and colleagues, "What really is the truth?"

1

The Problem

Pamela Stevens hung her wet overcoat behind the office door and glanced out her fourth floor window, noticing that the Washington Monument had disappeared in the fog. She walked to her desk and deposited her bagel and coffee right next to the problem.

I guess this is the day I gotta see Sam.

The file. She had started it three months earlier. As the lead reporter on Public Television System's "Salute to Darwin," a celebration of the 200th anniversary of the scientist's birthday scheduled for later in 2009, Pamela had traveled to several unusual places. She'd visited the Galapagos Islands and the Andes, as well as London, where she and her husband had taken a week away from their two small boys. She'd shot remarkable footage of animal habitats and interviewed some incredibly intelligent people on what Darwin's theories had proven about evolution, natural selection, and the origin of life. She knew that almost every corner of science was indebted to Darwin and his followers for proving that life is constantly changing and evolving to higher and more complex species and structures.

As she sipped her coffee, Pamela ran two fingers along the pendant hanging from her neck. It was a small piece of fossilized bone given to her in Africa, believed to be from an antelope-like creature millions of years old.

It would be an awesome two-hour celebration of the great man and the truths that he had proven. The special, scheduled to air in three months, would probably win Stevens and PTS another award, like the many that hung throughout her office.

Not bad for only being ten years out of school.

She focused again on the inch thick file, and frowned. Picking it up, she turned toward the window and opened it. Inside were many pages—some she'd written by hand, others she'd typed. Some pages had just a few notes. Others were full. And there were photocopies of several articles.

Pamela sighed and typed a message on her computer requesting a meeting for that afternoon.

Sam Hollis, Pamela's boss, had been a fixture at PTS for twenty-five years. An icon of the documentary industry, Sam had been everywhere and done everything. Twice. A brilliant African-American from New England, he'd begun his career tracing ancestries in western Africa and making vivid documentaries about the slave trade. His natural gift for video reporting had landed him at PTS, where he had risen quickly and was now the senior producer. Which was why Pamela needed to see him.

That afternoon Pamela entered Sam's large corner office, which was stuffed with memorabilia, photos and artifacts covering two tables and most of the floor from decades of traveling to the far corners of the earth. Sam smiled at his protégé and motioned her to join him at his desk, half-covered with unfinished projects. They shook hands.

"How was your New Year's?" the older man asked, pointing Pamela to a chair and moving several stacks so they could see each other.

"Fine." Pamela sat down, the file in her lap. "We had a few friends over. But then I had to leave on the third for Santiago. We taped the Andes segment for the Darwin documentary. I just got back yesterday."

"How was it?"

"Incredible. We got great shots of places where Darwin took long treks away from the ship in 1835. He was only 26."

"How is the video quality?"

"Excellent."

"Then you should be close to final editing." He smiled. "This may be another award winner."

Pamela knew Sam's compliment was genuine and intended for the whole team.

"Yes." She paused. "Actually, that's why I wanted to talk with you."

"What's up?"

"Well." Pamela took a deep breath. "We've produced a great documentary on Darwin, edifying his theories of Evolution and Natural Selection." She gently twirled the pendant with her right hand. "The problem is that I'm not sure his theories make any sense."

Sam's eyes widened. "What do you mean?"

Pamela slowly opened her file. "As I've gone through this process and traveled to all these places and interviewed all these people, the same thing keeps happening. Each of these brilliant people repeats some version of the 'fact' that Darwin's theories are well proven and beyond doubt. But when I ask them even the simplest question, there always seems to be a problem."

Sam scratched his head. "Problems with evolution? Like what?"

"Well, I'm talking about macro-evolution—they call it speciation. Not just that later generations of the same species are larger or slightly different. But the idea that one species actually changes into another. Take as an example the fossil record. Wouldn't it make sense that if all of the species we see on earth today evolved from earlier species, we would find the fossil remains of those in-between creatures? Like the ones that would be half way between a dinosaur and a bird, or between almost anything and something else?"

"Yes, of course."

"Well, there aren't any."

"Impossible," Sam said. He knitted his brows and swiveled in his chair.

"That's what I thought, too. But there really aren't. Well, there are a couple that Darwinists hold up as possibles. But compared to the tens of *millions* of fossils of species that existed earlier"—she raised the pendant slightly—"and either still exist today or are extinct, there really are none of the 'tweeners.'"

"How can that be?"

"I don't know. It even worried Darwin. He had to devote a whole chapter in *Origin of Species* to try to explain the problem away. I'm sure he thought that by 150 years later, we'd have found many of these fossils. But we haven't. Evolutionists today still call it a 'mystery.'"

The older man leaned back, accompanied by a creak from his chair. "I've never heard that. I find it hard to believe."

Pamela nodded and turned a page. "And here's a related one. There may have been life on earth for four or five billion years, but mostly it was bacteria. Then, about 550 million years ago, all of the basic body designs for all animals today suddenly appeared over a short period—about 20 million years. The first little animal traceable to us, through fish, amphibians, reptiles and mammals, suddenly showed up, fully formed. And then all through the fossil record, there are these disjointed 'jumps,' where nothing changes for a long time and then suddenly there is a new creature present, with none of the transitions that Darwin's theory would require."

"What do the scientists say about this?"

"They just repeat that the missing fossils will surely be found, as Darwin predicted."

"But I'm sure I've seen textbooks—when I was a kid, even—with those intermediate forms clearly displayed." Sam made an upward motion with his hands.

She nodded. "That's what I'm talking about. Everyone says that they 'must' exist. So far there are tens of millions of scientifically catalogued fossils, but few if any of the in between ones."

He sat in silence as Pamela continued. "And that's not all. In fact, there's lots more. Do you want to hear them?"

Sam nodded. He leaned forward and offered her a chocolate candy from a glass jar on his desk.

She smiled. "Thanks." Each unwrapped a candy and let it dissolve in a few moments of silence.

Pamela continued. "Okay. Here's one of my personal questions. It's the eye thing. How does vision *evolve*? I mean, how and why do all of the incredibly complex pieces—nerves, receptors, lenses, the optical part of the brain—all of that—start to fit together, long before there is any vision, to create what you

11

eventually need for an eye to function? What's the 'natural selection' going on, if there's no payoff of actual vision for a zillion years, to keep the process going? How does a lens 'learn' to focus, if there's nothing yet connected to it? And then how could this near miracle happen over and over again in so many different species and so many different places?"

Sam shook his head. "I don't know. I never thought about it. What do the scientists say?" He reached for another chocolate, unwrapped it and popped it into his mouth.

"They're not sure. They just say that it must have occurred over a long time. I mean, how would some blind thing just happen to develop all of the myriad parts necessary for vision while still blind? What trait would it have that would make it better, and therefore dominant, when it was still as blind as everything else? I don't get it."

Sam sat in silence, pondering her words. "Anything else?" He seemed to have lost the chipper spirit with which he'd greeted his friend.

Pamela turned a few pages. "As a sort of an aside, Darwin assumed that small building blocks, like bacteria, would be simple organisms from which more complex life forms evolved. But with modern microscopes, we now know that bacteria and other tiny creatures are actually incredibly complex, fine tuned, well-oiled machines. In fact, it's difficult to find any form of life on earth that isn't very, very complex. That suggests to me that everything started out complex, rather than evolving from something simpler. There just aren't any simple life forms anywhere."

Sam frowned and leaned forward again, his hands on the desk. "So what are you saying?"

Pamela's eye fell on a page in her folder. "Oh, here's one you should particularly like. Did you know that Darwin thought Negroes were 'tweeners,' a link between apes and humans? By higher humans he and his followers always meant Caucasians."

"What?" Sam took the page copied from Chapter 6 of *The Descent of Man* and read aloud.

> At some future period, not very distant as measured by centuries, the civilized races of man will almost certainly exterminate, and replace, the savage races throughout the world. At the same time the anthropomorphous apes, as Professor Schaaffhausen has remarked,[18] will no doubt be exterminated. The break between man and his nearest allies will then be wider, for it will intervene between man in a more civilized state, as we may hope, even than the Caucasian, and some ape as low as a baboon, instead of as now between the Negro or Australian and the gorilla.

He looked up at her, perplexed. "So Darwin was a racist?"

"Sort of, but not out of hate. Just 'science.' He predicted that whites would annihilate the 'savage races' in a few generations. Not because he wanted it—he was opposed to slavery—but because that would be the result of natural selection. How do you like being a link in the chain to better white people?"

Sam slammed the paper down. "That's absurd!"

Nodding and holding up her hands, Pamela said, "But that's the theory that we're about to celebrate in our documentary as being a proven fact."

"It's not true." Sam's anger had risen, along with his voice.

"And he said the same thing about women. Let me read from chapter 19 of the same book."

> The chief distinction in the intellectual powers of the two sexes is shewn by man's attaining to a higher eminence, in whatever he takes up, than can woman- whether requiring deep thought, reason, or imagination, or merely the use of the senses and hands. If two lists were made of the most eminent men and women in poetry, painting, sculpture, music (inclusive both of composition and performance), history, science, and philosophy, with half-a-dozen names under each subject, the two lists would not bear comparison. We may also infer, from the law of the deviation from averages, so well illustrated by Mr. Galton, in his work on Hereditary Genius, that if men are capable of a decided pre-eminence over women in many subjects, the average of mental power in man must be above that of woman.

"Ridiculous!"

"Can you think of any other white male we would honor who 'proved' that blacks and women are inferior to white males?"

Sam scowled his answer.

Pamela continued. "It's all part of evolutionary 'fact.' And everyone thinks evolution's true. So is it, or isn't it?"

"That part isn't."

"Are you a scientist?"

"No, but I know I'm not some link between apes and white people!"

"So with Darwin saying Negroes and women are less than human, and we can find no fossils of any in-between animals, and complex creatures appear almost at once, and no logic fits the evolution of something complex like vision, or flight, then which part of Darwin's theory of evolution *do* you agree with?"

Sam stood up and paced toward the window. His hands cut the air as he answered. "I don't know. I never thought about it. I just always thought that evolution was obvious."

"Right. Me, too. And if it's not? If it's wrong?"

Sam stopped and looked out the window. "Then...I don't know. Maybe we just 'happened.' Or something or someone created all of it." He turned back to Pamela. "I can't think of a good answer right now."

"But if someone or something created us, isn't that kind of defining?"

"What do you mean?"

"I mean," Pamela stood up and moved behind her chair, "that if all of this very complex world *were* created by someone, then wouldn't he, she or it have some ideas on how it ought to work? And what we ought to do and not do?"

Sam shook his head as he moved back to his desk. "Don't edge toward God and religion. Evolution sounds easier and better to me."

"But if it's clearly not true?"

"That may not matter. And how do we know, anyway? Maybe it is true."

"Well, maybe it is. But in ten minutes we shot it full of major holes, and no one out there seems to have answers that will plug them. Surely we ought to at least give equal time to other theories, when this one is so lame."

She could see the fury in her boss. He pointed his index finger as he spoke, "Listen, Pamela. You and I are not going to produce our own little show to question two hundred years of proven facts about evolution. Who are we to do that?"

"But they're *not* proven facts. That's what everyone thinks, because they don't ask the simplest questions. There are no evolutionary fossils, Sam!"

"Maybe there are, and we just haven't found them yet."

"Come on. You're starting to sound like a preacher, not a reporter, urging me to 'believe' in non-existent fossils. Maybe Darwinism is more of a religion than most religions. Just *believe*, and it's true."

Sam clasped the back of his chair with both hands, ignoring her chides. "I'm telling you that this documentary is going to air just like we planned it and just like you taped it. We can't just show up two hundred years later and doubt evolution. Can you imagine what that would mean? We'd have to question just about every theory we have if evolution isn't true, and I'm not about to stick my neck out to prove that Pamela Stevens knows more than Charles Darwin. Do you think we'd ever get a decent job in television again? We'd be finished, even if you're right."

She reached behind her neck, unclasped the pendant, and held it in her hand. She smiled but said forcefully "But so much of what Darwin and others call 'fact' is just untrue, or highly suspect. How can we add our documentary to the clamor of those congratulating him for being wrong? Haven't you always told me to seek and expose the truth?"

Sam swallowed. "Yes. Maybe you're right. You're certainly right about African-Americans and women. But if you kick over the foundation of evolution to explain where we all really came from, then what is there?"

"I don't know. That's what I want to ask."

"I'll tell you. It'll be God. All of the Godsquaders will pounce on this and use it to try to tell the rest of us how to live. Do you want that?"

"I don't know. I'm not a Godsquader. I just want the truth."

"Well, whatever you want, you'll get God. And I'd rather believe in evolution than God. Evolution doesn't tell you what to do."

"Even if it's *wrong*? If you're believing in a lie?"

"It's worked for all these years."

"Has it? You call what we've got today—working?"

Sam came around his chair and leaned toward Pamela with both hands on his desk. "Listen, Pamela. The bottom line is that you, I and PTS aren't going to rock this boat. Everyone believes that Darwin was a great man and that his theories are fact. So we'll just give everyone what they want in a spectacular, visually stimulating documentary on the great man's life, and call it a day. Okay? It's easier. And we won't get in trouble."

"Since when was our goal not to get in trouble? I thought our goal was truth in reporting."

"In this case, our goal is not to get in trouble. We'd never win. There are too many on the other side. And if we won, we'd just be helping the God people. It's too scary a thought."

"That's it?"

"That's it."

"Sam, I thought…"

The boss raised his hand. "Pamela, that's it."

Lie #1: Evolution is a fact.

Truth: Both Evolution (Macroevolution /Speciation) and Intelligent Design are theories which must be accepted or rejected on the best available evidence, and on faith.

http://www.apologeticspress.org/modules.php?name=Read&c
    at=5&itemid=2644
http://www.reasons.org
Perloff, James. *Tornado In A Junkyard: The Relentless Myth of Darwinism.* Arlington, MA.: Refuge Books, 1999.
Isaiah 40   Genesis 1-3
Acts 17: 24-28 Hebrews 11:3   Colossians 1: 15-17
Colson, Charles, and Nancy Pearcey. *Science and Evolution.* Wheaton, IL.: Tyndale House Publishers, 1999.
http://en.wikipedia.org/wiki/Charles_Darwin#The_Origin_of_
    Species
http://www.sjchurchofchrist.org/amino.shtml
Rana, Fazale, and Hugh Ross. *Origins of Life.* Colorado Springs, CO: Navpress, 2004.
http://www.icr.org/pubs/imp/imp-249.htm
http://www.str.org/free/commentaries/evolution/starligh.htm
http://www.str.org/free/commentaries/evolution/god_evol.htm
http://www.talkorigins.org/faqs/faq-intro-to-biology.html
http://www.goodschools.com/April19.htm
http://www.goodschools.com/descent_women.htm

For the latest updates go to www.tenliesandtentruths.com

Notes:

Ten Lies and Ten Truths

2

History

Harrison Gillies sat alone in the teacher's lounge of the prestigious public high school grading English essays. Paintings donated by the Art Department, an oriental rug, and a couple of decades' accumulation of furniture lifted the room beyond its institutional beginnings. Gillies, nearing retirement, was slightly overweight. In an earlier era, he would have been smoking a pipe. From his comfortable chair by the window, he glanced at the clock, expecting the door to open any minute, as it did about this time on most Monday afternoons.

The latch clicked and his younger colleague, Sandra Murphy, walked in carrying file folders and papers. She smiled and went to the counter by the sink to pour hot water. They enjoyed having tea together during their mutual free period.

"Looks like we finally got them," she said, holding up the papers. "This ought to silence them once and for all."

"Nice to see you, too." Gillies smiled. "When are you going to learn that in the South we say 'Hello' or 'How are you?' before launching into a declarative sentence?"

She smiled, put the papers under her arm, and picked up the oversize mugs. He put the essays on a table next to his chair and took the warm mug she offered.

She stood in front of his chair. "All right. Harrison, how are y'all?"

"Fine, thank you. But just because I'm heavy doesn't mean I'm plural."

"Sorry. I thought the term applied universally."

"No, it's much more complex than the simple 'you'. You'll get the hang of it one day."

She laughed. "Actually, when I call home it slips out sometimes. They're always aghast. And I like grits, too."

"There's hope. But now that we've reminded you to 'whittle and spit' a little, what were you talking about when you came in?" He sipped his tea and motioned her to the sofa on the other side of the table.

"Here, I brought you a copy." Murphy handed him three pages and sat on the sofa. Moving the pencil she was carrying to the table, she used both hands to pull back her light blond hair. "The Supreme Court just issued a ruling that should finally make things clear."

Gillies adjusted his glasses. "Let me see." He read aloud.

FOR IMMEDIATE RELEASE

Washington, DC (AP). June 17, 2011. In a 5 to 4 decision, the U.S. Supreme Court ruled today that the Declaration of Independence, along with President Washington's Inauguration and Farewell Addresses, may no longer be displayed or read in public schools.

Citing the First Amendment, the court ruled that because there is a reference to God in each document, it is a violation of the Constitution's prescribed separation of church and state to include the Declaration of Independence or Washington's speeches in public education.

In addition, the display of the documents in government buildings and in other facilities supported with federal funds is also banned.

Gillies lowered the press release into his lap and looked over at his colleague. "This is pretty strong."

She eased back into the cushions on the sofa. "Yes, thank goodness."

Each of them took a sip, and Gillies picked up the press release.

Writing for the majority, Chief Justice Diane Timmons-Fulton ruled that "American school-children will no longer be subjected to the narrow and bigoted view that the male imaged Judeo-Christian God, some other god, or any other religious construction was involved in the creation of our country."

Speaking of George Washington and the other Founding Fathers, the Chief Justice wrote, "Either they were misguided at the time, or they did not foresee the implications of their personal beliefs on future generations. In either case, the court cannot allow words written over 200 years ago to improperly influence the citizens of our nation to believe in God, or in any other specific divine being."

Federal, state and local governments will have one month to remove all copies of the documents from public buildings, and local school

boards will have a year to acquire new history
books that do not explicitly quote the texts.

"I suppose your History Department will be investing in new
textbooks."

"Yes, though the ones we've been using for years don't
mention those speeches by Washington."

He smiled and turned slightly in his chair. "Why are you so
strident about this ruling?"

"Harrison, come on! We've both been on the receiving end
of those parents' e-mails and conferences where they want us to
allow students to say anything about their faith here at school. If
we did that, we'd have Christians berating Jews, Jews hating
Muslims, and all of them ganging up on the atheists. The only safe
way is to allow none of it. Keep all religions out of school. And
clearly the Constitution requires it."

Gillies frowned and took another sip of tea before reading
the second page.

In writing the minority dissent, Justice
Wilton Thrower argued that "it would take many
pages of single spaced entries just to list all
of the public documents in which the Founding
Fathers explicitly mentioned the Judeo-Christian
God, His Son Jesus Christ, and their dependence
on Him for guiding them through the ordeal of
birthing this unique nation. Not only is this ban
historically inaccurate, but it also strikes a
blow to the one true Foundation of our country."

Justice Thrower pointed out that the First
Amendment was specifically written to prevent

Congress from "establishing" a central religion for the nation, that it guarantees free expression on all religious issues, and that the term "Separation of Church and State" never appears in the Constitution or the Bill of Rights.

"Denying our nation's dependence on God has become a gross distortion of the intent of the Founders. They always *encouraged* the influence of religious thought in public policy.

"In addition, until the 1970s, generations of public school children grew up reading these two important speeches by our first and greatest President. In them Washington gives the formula for the continuing success, safety, and prosperity of our nation, the key element of which is an abiding belief in God and adherence to His commandments."

He looked up. "What do you think of that?"

She shrugged. "It doesn't matter what I think. The Constitution creates a wall between church and state. Period."

Her older mentor nodded. "Justice Thrower says it doesn't, and that the First Amendment is only talking about Congress establishing a state religion."

"Well, if anyone talks about God in a public school, that's exactly what they're doing."

"Is it? Are we Congress? We're a school."

"How can you say that? You've complained about these religious fanatics as many times as I have."

Gillies laughed and set the papers in his lap. "Yes. I know. But you're the historian. Isn't what President Washington said a matter of history?"

"Yes, but it shouldn't be used to brainwash people today."

"It's history."

"And history shows us what happens when religion runs wild."

"Are you saying that's what happened during the American Revolution?"

She glared at him. "You know what I mean. We can't have religion at this school."

"What if we did open up—let all the students say whatever they wanted? Instead of excluding all religions in the name of not offending anyone, what if we just let everyone speak their mind?"

"We'd have chaos!"

"But aren't we in the business of education? The interchange of ideas? Haven't you and I been on the frontlines of supporting diversity?"

"Some students would be hurt. It wouldn't be right."

"By words? Sandra, I teach English. If the school itself doesn't take sides, and insures that no one is unduly coercive, isn't that the kind of dialogue we want?"

She shook her head. "Not about religion. Not with fundamentalist bigots."

"Sounds like diversity-lite." He picked up the paper. "Let me finish it."

People for Truth in Government, which brought the original lawsuit, issued a statement foreseeing the same result in a similar suit to overturn the national motto, "In God We Trust," which is found on the nation's currency. The statement also pointed out that one of Justice Thrower's maternal ancestors owned slaves in South Carolina in the nineteenth century, and that both his uncle and grandfather were ministers, "so it is no surprise that Justice Thrower would be swayed on this issue. We are delighted that the majority instead held to truth and logic."

Chief Justice Timmons-Fulton concluded her ruling by stating that "since the United States did not officially exist until the Constitution was ratified in 1788, any ex-officio meetings, writings or communications which may have occurred in the years prior to that date, including the 1776 gathering in Philadelphia to write the Declaration of Independence, cannot be given any official status, and so it is only proper that this group's narrow belief in God be stricken from the nation's historic record and be accorded no particular significance.

"In addition, while President Washington certainly helped establish the nation and governed reasonably well in its early years, it is precisely this lasting prestige which today makes it inappropriate for others to force his antiquated views about God on later generations. Unsuspecting schoolchildren might be encouraged

to believe that God actually exists simply
because George Washington apparently believed so.
This would be a great tragedy."

He put down the pages. "You're right. That's pretty clear."

She tapped her finger on the mahogany coffee table in front
of the sofa. "So the next time a parent, or even a student,
complains that we don't allow the open expression of ideas on
faith, religion, or whatever, we'll just give them a copy of this and
tell them that we're following the law." She turned to face him.
"And I know you agree with me. You must!"

He leaned forward and looked down at the papers. "Yes, I
suppose you're right."

"Sometimes I think you ask me questions just to get me
going, to practice your Socratic teaching method. But I know
you."

"I admit, I do like playing Devil's advocate. Forty years of
teaching teenagers." He leaned back and looked out the window.
"But there is something about this that bothers me." Gillies
scratched his face, then wrapped his hands around the mug and
held it in his lap. "When I was a graduate student at the
University of London in the 70s, a Soviet student lived in my
dorm. He was one of the few allowed to study abroad in those
days. He was a little older than me, and much smarter. Over
several months we became friends."

He paused, his mind obviously on the past.

"I don't know how it came up. Maybe an anniversary of
World War II. Anyway, he didn't believe that his country had
invaded Poland a few weeks following Germany in 1939."

"The Molotov-Ribbentrop Pact. Hitler and Stalin divided Poland on paper in August, and invaded in September. And then Stalin took the Baltic states for good measure as well."

He nodded and looked her way. "A-plus, historian. But, you see, Sergey had no knowledge of it. In fact, he got angry with me for even suggesting that his country could do something so despicable as to invade a peaceful neighbor. He was absolutely sure I was wrong."

She shrugged her shoulders. "But you were right. Facts are facts."

"Not to Sergey. He only knew the facts that Stalin had rewritten. The government didn't want its people to know the real facts—for the greater good of 'socialist reality.' In just one generation, Stalin's rewrite won, and the truth was lost to all but a handful of people."

Sandra was silent. "But surely you don't equate what Stalin did to this?"

He smiled. "Stalin wasn't as eloquent."

"Come on." She dismissed his words with a wave of her hand.

He sat up and turned all the way to face her. "No, I'm serious. You and I might agree with the outcome for now. But our own government has just ruled that the real truth can no longer be taught. In a generation, it, too, will be gone and forgotten. I can imagine some young American in London in twenty years arguing that President Washington could never have believed in God. That it would be impossible because Washington never mentioned God in his writing or his speeches."

"Harrison, come on. That could never happen here."

"Why?" He held her eyes.

"Because this is America."

Lie #2: The Founding Fathers did not acknowledge God's important role in the founding of this nation.

Truth: The majority of the Founding Fathers were Christians or Deists who believed in God and actively gave Him credit for acting in their daily lives and for founding this nation. They based America's laws on Biblical laws, quoted scripture in their writings and debates, and fully expected the nation to maintain its Christian heritage so that morality and ethics would make the rule of law possible.

Barton, David. *Original Intent: The Courts, the Constitution, & Religion.* Aledo, Texas: WallBuilder Press, 1996.
http://www.eadshome.com/ChiefExecutive.htm
http://www.wallbuilders.com/resources/search/historicalwritings.php
http://www.federalist.com
DeMar, Gary. *America's Christian History.* Atlanta: American Vision, Inc., 1993.
DeMar, Gary. *You've Heard It Said.* Brentwood, Tenn.: Wolgemuth & Hyatt, 1991.
http://www.eppc.org/publications/pubID.2323/pub_detail.asp
Psalm 33:12   Proverbs 14:34
Jeremiah 18:7-10   Isaiah 33:22
http://www.americanvision.org
Lapin, Rabbi Daniel. *America's Real War.* Sisters, OR.: Multnomah Publishers, 1999.
http://www.str.org/free/commentaries/social_issues/churchan.htm

For the latest updates go to www.tenliesandtentruths.com

Notes:

3

Words

Mike Beal wore a dark blue suit, white shirt and red tie. Tall and handsome with a bit of gray dusting his auburn hair, the prosecutor presented an imposing figure. He rose from his seat in the paneled courtroom. Looking purposefully at the jury members seated in their box, he strode toward the State's star witness.

Mary Alexander, in her mid-twenties, attractive, with chestnut brown hair, wore a stylish pale blue dress and a single strand of pearls.

Beal stood next to her, his hand on the witness box rail, his face visible to the jury. "Ms. Alexander, please state your full name and address for the record."

"Mary C. Alexander. 310 Cotter Lane."

"And where do you work?"

"In Midtown, at Coles and Company. I'm an executive assistant."

"All right. Thank you. Now I'd like you to tell us, please, in your own words what happened to you and your baby almost ten months ago on the morning of October 19th."

Mary paused for a moment before speaking, all the while clasping her hands tightly in her lap.

"I...I left my office at 9:30 to go to a doctor's appointment—the doctor's office is near our office. I was walking up Tenth Street on the north side—on the sidewalk, I mean. When I got to

Fulmer, I waited for the light to change, and then I started into the crosswalk."

She hesitated, glancing from Beal to the judge, who was looking down benevolently from her slightly raised position next to the witness stand.

"What happened then?" the prosecutor encouraged.

"Well, there was yelling from a car stopped across the intersection on Fulmer. I glanced that way and two men jumped out, raising their hands and yelling at each other."

"Do you see one of those men here in the courtroom this morning?"

"Yes. That's one of them. Mr. Sanchez."

"Let the record show that the witness is pointing to Mr. Raymond Sanchez, the defendant."

Sanchez, seated at the defendant's table with his two court-appointed attorneys, stared at her. He was wearing what appeared to be a recently purchased but ill-fitting gray suit and green tie.

Beal nodded for Mary to continue.

"They were yelling so loudly that everyone just sort of stopped and looked at them. The one on the passenger side suddenly ran across the intersection toward us. Just then the driver—Mr. Sanchez—started shooting at him with a gun—a pistol." Her hands increased their wringing motion. "I guess the passenger heard the first shot and tried to dodge, so he darted to the right and then to the left. He ran past me. But...but Mr. Sanchez fired again, and the bullet hit me."

"Where?"

"In the stomach." She touched the spot on her side. "I felt a sharp pain, and I saw blood. I turned back to the sidewalk, but I fell in the street. People were screaming and running. I think Mr. Sanchez fired a couple more times. It gets pretty blurry after that."

"All right," Beal said, in a soothing tone. "You're doing fine." He had glanced at the jury during her testimony and noticed the attention with which they were following her story. "What's the next thing you remember?"

"I know that an ambulance came. Lots of sirens. People were trying to help me. One man used his shirt to try to stop the bleeding. I guess I passed out, because the next thing I recall was being in the hospital bed."

"After the operation?"

"Yes. It must have been several hours later. There were bandages on the wound. I was still pretty woozy."

"And where was your baby?"

"She...she wasn't there." Mary looked down and appeared to be close to tears.

"What had happened to her?"

"They told me later that the bullet would have passed pretty cleanly through me, but because I was pregnant, it hit the baby's head and exploded."

There was silence in the court for a few moments.

"And killed her?"

Mary nodded.

"I know this is difficult. We'll have expert testimony later, but did they say that they tried to save her?"

Tears were now streaming down Mary's cheeks. She gasped, "Yes."

"And at 25 weeks, your baby was probably viable, given all that medical science can do now." Beal handed her a handkerchief.

Mary just nodded, wiping her eyes.

"I'm sorry. No more questions. Thank you, Mary. Now I think Mr. Philips probably has some questions for you."

All eyes in the courtroom turned to the defendant's table. After a few moments of silently studying notes on a legal pad, Jim Philips rose and nodded pleasantly to Mary Alexander. Younger and shorter than the prosecutor, Philips felt around in several pockets of his blue suit until he found a pen, made one short note on his pad, and then walked toward the witness. He stopped in the middle of the room, just in front of the judge.

"Good morning, Ms. Alexander. I'm sorry that you had to go through that again. You did a good job."

She nodded and looked at him.

"As you know, I'm Jim Philips. Ms. Tobin and I are representing Mr. Sanchez."

"Yes," she said.

"And he is on trial for manslaughter. For unintentionally killing your unborn baby. He's already been tried and found guilty for the other things he did that morning following the drug deal that went bad. None of that is in dispute. The only thing we're here to try him on today is causing the death of your baby. Whatever the outcome of the trial, do you think that Mr. Sanchez meant harm to either you or your baby?"

"Objection," Prosecutor Beal said, rising from his chair. "Ms. Alexander's opinion on that matter is not relevant."

Philips answered, "Your honor, I believe that intent is a relevant factor in a manslaughter case, and I think that Ms. Alexander's opinion is very relevant.".

"I'll allow it," the judge responded. "Please answer Mr. Philips' question."

"No, I guess not. Not ahead of time. But he shouldn't have shot at me!"

Philips continued. "Yes. I understand. By shooting at his former partner, whom he intended to harm but didn't, he injured you and fatally wounded your baby. He wanted to hurt his partner, not you. Yet he's here today because he accidentally hit you."

"Objection."

"Sustained. Mr. Philips, it will be the jury's decision, not yours, about whether this event was a reckless act of endangerment or an accident. The jury will disregard Mr. Philips' characterization. Where are you going with this line of questions, Mr. Philips?"

Facing the gray haired veteran on the bench, Philips deferred. "Sorry, your honor. I just wanted to establish that Mr. Sanchez did not intend to harm Ms. Alexander or her baby."

"Go on."

"Yes. Now, Ms. Alexander, on the morning in question, where did you say that you were going as you were walking on Tenth Street?"

"Objection. Where she was going is not relevant."

The judge looked at Beal. "I'll allow it. But," turning to Philips, "please make your point quickly." She then nodded to the witness and smiled.

Mary looked down, then up at Philips. "I was going to Doctor Slaton's office."

"And is Doctor Slaton your regular doctor, or was he your obstetrician?"

A long pause. "Neither."

"And so why were you going to Dr. Slaton's office that morning?"

"To...to have an abortion."

There was a stir in the courtroom. Prosecutor Beal looked impassively toward his witness. Several of the jurors glanced at each other. The judge eventually pounded her gavel. "Order. Ladies and gentlemen, we must have order or we cannot proceed."

Jim Philips continued. "So you were on your way that morning to have your baby killed?"

"Objection!"

"Sustained."

"But, your honor, what else would you call it? She was on the way to kill her baby when Mr. Sanchez unintentionally did the same thing."

"Abortion," the judge scowled at the young defense attorney. "She was on the way to have an abortion. Not to 'kill her baby.' "

"What difference does it make to the baby in the words that we use?"

"Mr. Philips, we're not here to try Ms. Alexander's legal right to an abortion. Do you have any more questions for her that are relevant to Mr. Sanchez's case?"

Philips turned back to the witness. "Why were you going to abort your daughter, Ms. Alexander?"

"Objection!"

"Mr. Philips, I've warned you not to follow that line. Do you want me to hold you in contempt of court?"

"But intent is relevant in a manslaughter case. We think it's relevant that if Mr. Sanchez had not fired his pistol that morning, Ms. Alexander's baby would have been dead an hour later, anyway. That was Ms. Alexander's intent. To kill her baby. The baby is dead either way, but the only difference is that in one case, the mother intended it and in the other case Mr. Sanchez did not. To lock Mr. Sanchez away for twenty years for doing what Ms. Alexander was on her way to do anyway seems preposterous."

"The jury will disregard everything that Mr. Philips just said." Turning to the defense attorney, the judge scowled. "Mr. Philips, if a doctor takes the life of a terminally ill patient or a prison guard murders an inmate on death row, it is still a crime. The eventual fate of the victim is not an issue."

"Yes, your honor, but in those analogies the person most like the doctor or the prison guard would be Ms. Alexander, because she *intended* to kill the victim. Mr. Sanchez did not."

"Mr. Philips, you'll stop this, or I'll declare a mistrial."

"All right." Turning to Mary again, he said. "Ms. Alexander, I'm sincerely sorry to ask you these questions, but since Mr. Sanchez will spend most of the rest of his life in jail if he is found guilty, it's very important that we understand as much as possible."

She nodded but said nothing.

He looked down at his notes, took a couple of steps and looked at the jury. "Given where you were going at the time of the incident, had you been awake when you arrived at the hospital, would you have Okayed the doctors' work on your daughter, or would you have withheld permission to try to save her life?"

"Objection!"

"Your honor, I'm trying to establish that even after the incident, had Ms. Alexander been awake, her intent would have been for the baby not to live."

"One more question like that, and you're finished here. Do you understand?"

"But if not immediately relevant to the act itself, certainly these questions are important as to the extenuating circumstances surrounding the event."

"Mr. Philips, we're not here to discuss what *might* have happened. We're here to find out what actually did happen."

Jim Philips looked at the judge, who continued to scowl. He glanced down at his notes and over to his client. Then he looked back at Mary Alexander, nodded and smiled.

"Thank you, Ms. Alexander. No more questions."

Another full day of expert testimony and eyewitness accounts followed. Finally, the testimony ended, the prosecutor and defense attorney made their final summations, and the case went to the jury.

After four hours of deliberation, the foreman notified the judge that they had reached a verdict. Twenty minutes later, the court reconvened.

With everyone seated, the judge addressed the foreman, "Has the jury reached a verdict?"

He stood. "Yes your honor, we have."

"All right, then, what say you?"

Ten Lies and Ten Truths

Lie #3: Abortion is not murder.

Truth: Abortion is the murder of a living human being.

http://www.silentnomoreawareness.org/
Genesis 9:6
http://www.str.org/free/commentaries/abortion/feticide.htm
http://lifecommercials.com
http://www.linda.net/titles.html
Psalm 139
http://withchrist.org/abortion.htm
Luke 1:15 & 41
http://www.catholiceducation.org/articles/abortion/ab0005.html
http://www.huppi.com/kangaroo/L-abortion.htm
http://www.str.org/free/commentaries/abortion/murderok.htm
http://abortionismurder.org/notconvinced.shtml

For the latest updates go to www.tenliesandtentruths.com

Notes:

4

The Plane Trip

Diane Woods—well, that was her old African-American name. At age twenty-eight, she would soon be assuming a new name in a new country. Diane buckled herself into the window seat for the one-hour flight from London's Heathrow Airport to Frankfurt, Germany. It was a roundabout itinerary, but she and her husband had spent an hour online piecing together a string of flights so that she could use a frequent flier ticket. It was almost time for departure and she hoped there wouldn't be a passenger in the seat next to her. She wanted to stretch out and relax after her sleepless overnight flight from Washington. She held a pillow in her lap and was about to place it against the bulkhead when a small woman who might be her same age appeared in the aisle looking a little confused.

In broken English the woman, who had dark skin, but not as dark as Diane's, said, "Pardon, please. Is this Eighteen B?"

Diane lifted her magazine from the adjoining seat. "Yes. Yes it is."

"Oh, good. I think I am to sit here." She offered her ticket to Diane, who, somewhat startled, took it, noted the seat assignment, and nodded.

"Yes, this is it."

The woman placed her small bag on the floor between them and collapsed into the seat. She closed her eyes, and it appeared to Diane that her neighbor might be praying, since her lips moved but her eyes remained shut.

When the woman opened her eyes, Diane smiled and tried to make conversation. "A long flight?"

The woman returned her smile. "Not too long. The next after this is longer. To America! We missed our flight this morning, they put me on another one, and now I have to go to Frankfurt to connect. But I've just been praying for my husband."

"Where is he?"

"Still back home." She pointed behind her. "The officials wouldn't let him leave our country this morning. They said that his papers were not in order, even though we have worked on them for months. I didn't want to leave, but we talked, and he said it is better for me to go. He will stay behind and try to straighten it out. But I am concerned for him."

"Where are you from?" Diane asked, still smiling.

The woman told her.

"Oh, goodness. That's where I'm going! Isn't that interesting? Maybe you can tell me about it."

Her companion pulled back a little. A questioning look appeared on her face. "You are an American? Why do you go there?"

Before Diane could answer, the captain made the usual takeoff announcement. She helped her new seatmate find the end of her seatbelt. "My husband found a job there as a chemical engineer for three years. We're moving away from American stereotypes and starting a new life."

"Oh, I see." But her seatmate looked confused.

The plane pushed back from the gate with a slight jerk. Diane felt her heart race as she gripped the armrests.

"Are you all right?" her new companion asked.

"Uh, yes. I just don't like flying."

"Oh." She smiled, her eyes bright. "This morning was my first time in an airplane."

They turned to face forward and sat in silence as the plane taxied out to the runway. Once they were airborne and the noise subsided, Diane released one hand, touched the woman's arm, smiled, and said, "My name is Diane."

Her companion nodded back. "My name is Aisha."

"You are brave."

Aisha smiled and shook her head. "Not really."

"Do you have any children?"

"No, not yet. We hope to in America. You?"

Diane answered. "No. We've only been married two years. We've both had careers. I hope to continue mine. I've been a paralegal, and of course, in our new country, I imagine I'll have to learn everything over again. Luckily my husband's engineering expertise is useful almost anywhere."

"Yes. Yes. My husband is also an engineer. We think that may be why he had trouble today. They don't want him to leave. I think it will be a big problem."

"I'm sure it will be okay. They can't detain him indefinitely if he has the correct papers."

Aisha looked at her quizzically.

"Does he have a job in America?" Diane asked.

Aisha shook her head. "No, but several families are sponsoring us, in Nashville. When we get to America, I'm sure that he will get a job. He is very smart."

"Why Nashville?"

"A church is helping us. You see, we are Christians now, and everyone at home started to argue with us and take from us. We lost our apartment. I lost my job as a teacher. They kept my husband at the plant but lowered his pay. Our families refused to see us. Someone told my husband that they will kill us."

Diane frowned. "That must be a tiny fundamentalist minority. I checked, and your country has religious freedom and tolerance."

Aisha looked at her again, then smiled and shook her head. "Yes, freedom if you are Muslim. Everyone else they despise. I know. I grew up Muslim."

"That's interesting. I grew up Christian in D.C. Or at least my parents were Christians. My husband and I recently converted to Islam. So I suppose you could say that we're trading places with you."

Aisha did not smile this time. "You converted from Christianity to Islam? Why?"

Diane shifted in her seat and tapped the armrest as she spoke. "Because we were tired of the hypocrisy of Christian America, always proclaiming equality, but only meaning it for white men, not for women or for African-Americans. My husband was turned away from a white church when he was in college. He says that Christianity is only for the ruling elite in America, and we got sick of it. He decided to worship God as a Muslim instead, and I joined him." She shrugged. "It's the same God. We just don't want all of the church crap that comes along with it in America."

"Hmm. So you think you will have a better life as a Muslim woman, and that is why you converted?"

48

"Yes," Diane answered, "and because we like the structure of Islam. Do certain things at certain times, help the poor, and you'll be OK. Pretty easy to understand. Follow Allah's rules, do good deeds, and you'll be all right."

"Are you sure? Islam doesn't guarantee that. It just says that Allah *might* like you if you do those things. It's totally up to his whim. And what if you miss something important? What do you do?"

"You offset it with more good deeds. Or you take an extra pilgrimage. "

"Well, you certainly understand what we were taught from childhood, that we have to try hard all our lives to please Allah, and hope that he likes what we do."

"Yes, I like that kind of structure."

"You will learn a lot about structure as a woman in our country."

"What do you mean?"

Aisha smiled. "You will see. Besides the dress, women are always second-class. We cannot worship with our husbands. We cannot start businesses on our own. We are not encouraged to continue our education. Divorce is a terrible thing for a woman. In one way we *are* equal to men: we can vote, but since there is only one party and one ruling group, our votes are as worthless as the men's."

"You don't make it sound very inviting," Diane frowned. "Is that why you're leaving? Because of the inequality?"

The flight attendants arrived with the beverage cart. After they moved further down the aisle, Aisha sipped her coffee without answering for a few moments. Finally she lowered the cup to her lap and turned slightly toward her American neighbor.

"No. I guess you get used to all that. I think it is worse in some Muslim countries. Better in others. No, the reason we are leaving is because we are being persecuted for our faith. As I told you, we have lost everything. We are threatened. Others have been beaten. Did that happen to you in America when you became a Muslim?"

"No. Of course not." Diane patted her hand. "What happened to you sounds terrible. I had no idea. But, again, surely that is a tiny minority of extremists, not true Islam."

"Actually, persecution *is* the true teaching of Islam. The 'structure,' as you put it, has no place for Muslims who convert from the faith. Were it not for the façade of Western laws in our country, the Koran itself says that we should be killed."

There was more silence. Finally, Diane asked, "Given all of that pressure, how and why did you become a Christian?"

Aisha smiled. "Because for the first time in our lives we heard about love. I mean about God's love. His love for us. You see, the Koran has 99 descriptions of Allah, but none of them is love. He is all-powerful, aloof, judgmental, all knowing. But not loving. According to the Koran, Allah made us and we are his servants. He would never want a friendly relationship with us. So when we heard on the radio that God loves us and wants a relationship with us, it was very new and exciting."

The plane suddenly encountered turbulence and Diane froze. She turned and looked out the window. Everything appeared to be all right. She turned again to her companion, but continued to grip the armrest between them. "On the radio?"

"Yes. It's against the law to talk about Christianity in our country except inside the few churches that the government allows to exist. There are no Christian books in the library or bookstores, and of course, nothing about Christianity on the state run television or radio. We first heard about God's love on the short wave radio, and then we studied it on the Internet. It was like a whole new world for us. We wanted to tell others, but we were afraid."

Now Diane leaned forward. "Wait a minute. The Christian God is not just about love. He is also judgmental, just like Allah. I know all about those rules. Look at the Ten Commandments. Look at all the rules in the Old Testament. There's no difference."

Aisha's smile turned into a grin. "Oh, yes, of course. He made us, so He naturally has rules for us to live by, for our own good. But here are the differences, the things that spoke so deeply to my husband and me. God the Father, unlike Allah, longs for a true relationship with us. He walked with Adam and Eve. He is the joyful father running to meet his prodigal son. Allah would never do that. God wants us to be in fellowship with Him.

"But here's the most amazing thing. God made a way of deliverance for us when we fail. In Islam, failure means to try harder, to do more, and to hope that you can please Allah. You never know. You just try and try. But God has instead provided the way out of our failures, our sins. He loves us so much that He had his son Jesus die in our place, for the things you and I have done that separate us from Him. So that we can return to Him. So that we will spend eternity with Him. We can't possibly do that ourselves. Allah wants us to keep trying, like it's a game with a score, but we never know if we've scored enough. God instead lifts us up in His arms, loving us because, if we repent and believe, Jesus has already done what we can never do."

Diane leaned back in her seat and looked out the window again.

Aisha continued, a smile lighting her face. "That's why we're so excited. God loves us! Allah never did and never will. Isn't that incredible?"

"I...guess."

"And that frees us. Persecution is bad, but it's not the end. I pray that my husband gets out and joins me. I want to grow old with him. But even if that doesn't happen, I know that God loves both of us, that He has a plan for us, and that we'll see each other again in heaven. We're free to love...to love everyone, even the ones who persecute us."

Diane shook her head. "You must have been told about a different Christianity than I grew up with."

"Why?"

"Well, I guess there was some joy...in my mama's church. But then there are all the rules against everything from dancing to drinking to buying stuff on Sundays. And that 'All men are created equal' line, as long as you're not a woman or black. And white Christians owning slaves, and big rich churches turning away the homeless. I just get sick of all that."

Aisha listened and frowned slightly. "Forgive me. I have never been to America, so of course I don't know. But those things sound like what people do, not what Christianity teaches. Or what Jesus himself would do."

"It's all the same."

"Again, forgive me, but I have to disagree. In America I think that people have failed to live up to the teaching of the faith, that we are all created in the image of God, and that we should love each other as God loves us. In our country, the teaching itself is that Allah wants us to keep trying to please him, and to do so we have to live according to rules and laws that have nothing to do with love. In your country, the ideal is there, like a beacon, to turn you back to a relationship with God—that is uplifting. In our country, the ideal is a long set of rules that can never be changed—that keep people down. So it's not the same. God is not Allah...thank God!"

Diane shook her head again. "You have faith like a small child. But it's not that simple."

Aisha nodded. "Maybe it is. I know that you will see for yourself what I have been talking about."

"And I think that you will see the hypocrisy in America."

"Yes, probably. And I will try, with God's help, to shine the light of His true teaching into those situations."

"Good luck."

Aisha lowered her eyes, then looked up at her companion. "Diane, for your sake, don't try to change anything in my country."

Diane looked at her and frowned.

"And keep your American passport with you. You may decide that Allah is not who you think he is. If you decide to return to God, you won't be able to do that where you are going."

"I—uh—okay. Thank you."

The engine noise reduced as the plane began its descent. Diane looked around quickly and then tightened her seatbelt.

"We will be all right," Aisha said. "God is in charge of this airplane, and of everything else."

"I hope so. And I hope that your husband is able to join you soon. Could...could I have his address, in case we can help?"

"Yes, but I don't recommend that you visit him. It could make life very difficult for you there."

Diane frowned again. "Just for talking to him? We'll see about that."

The Plane Trip

Ten Lies and Ten Truths

Lie #4: God and Allah are the same.

Truth: Though both faiths are monotheistic, Allah is an aloof creator who rules over people with random and unpredictable judgments, meaning that his followers must obey rules and do good deeds to earn his benevolence. God the Father is not aloof, but instead created us to have a relationship with Him and loves us so much that He gave His only son Jesus to atone for the sins of all who believe. We cannot earn this salvation. We are not saved by keeping rules or by our own works, but by His grace.

Ben Abraham, Isaac. *Islam, Terrorism and Your Future.* Cedar
        Hill Press, 2002.
http://www.gospelcom.net/rbc/questions/answer/religion/islam/god
        character.xml/
Acts 17:22-34
http://www.breadsite.org/in200214.htm
http://www.submission.org/
Luke 15:11-32
http://www.christian-witness.org/islam/imi_islam.html

For the latest updates go to www.tenliesandtentruths.com

Notes:

Ten Lies and Ten Truths

5

The Vote

"There they are," Dylan said to Ashley, as they hurried into the international arrivals area at the Los Angeles Airport.

Smiling broadly, Ashley hugged Judith, her old friend from Australia. "It's so good to see you!"

Ten years earlier, before they were married, Dylan and Ashley Ibitson had been American graduate students in Oxford, and Judith had been Ashley's Australian roommate.

"You don't look a day older." Dylan smiled as he shook Thomas' hand.

When Judith and her Oxford boyfriend, Thomas Gurling, were married in Australia two years after graduation, the Ibitsons, also newlyweds, had flown out for the wedding. In the intervening eight years and two children apiece, the couples had not been as close. But now the Australians had arrived in the U.S. so that Judith could attend a conference at the start of the new year.

"Only you two would fly on New Year's Eve," Ashley said, as she hugged Thomas.

"Fares on the hyperplanes are going up in 2035," Judith explained, "so we decided to spend a couple of extra days with our favorite Yanks. We hope you don't mind having us."

"Of course not! We love it. I just wish you could have brought Jonathon and Amy."

"They'll be just as happy with their grandparents. And Mom and Dad are used to taking care of Jonathon," Thomas said. "So, how are you two?"

"We're great. Let's get your luggage to the car. We're on a bit of a tight schedule," Dylan added, as he reached for one of the suitcases.

"The Vote?" Thomas asked.

"Yes."

"That's another reason we wanted to arrive today. We've read about it for years, but we wanted to see how it works in action, so to speak."

With a suitcase in each hand, Dylan headed for the exit. "It's always interesting. Hopefully we'll make it home in time for you to see it all."

"Lead on," Judith said, as the four friends continued to the car.

Ninety minutes later the two couples were relaxing in the Ibitsons' den. The Gurlings had unpacked and freshened up, handed out gifts to the kids, and been shown the latest improvements to the back yard landscaping. Now, drinks in hand, the four friends were seated around the television/family computer in two comfortable chairs and a sofa.

"How are Jonathon and Amy?" Ashley asked.

"Amy at three never stops asking questions," Judith replied. "And she certainly knows how to get her way with her father."

Thomas smiled. "And Jonathon, now that he's six, is doing well in school, even with his Mosaic Down's Syndrome."

Ashley nodded. "We were so concerned about him when he was born."

"Yes. Jonathon has certainly taught us patience that we didn't know we had. And love."

They spent the next thirty minutes catching up on family and old friends. As four o'clock approached, it was inevitable that The Vote should come up.

"So," Thomas said, leaning forward from the sofa and putting his drink on the coffee table in front of him, "How does it actually work?"

Dylan glanced from the TV to his watch, and then back to his Australian friend. "In about ten minutes the process will start, as it does every New Year's Eve afternoon. We'll vote instantaneously on, I don't know, maybe twenty or thirty issues that will then be implemented for 2035."

"Who decides what will be voted on?" Judith asked.

Ashley responded. "During November and December anyone can place an issue at The Vote website. The rest of us review the proposals and add our support for nomination. If an issue receives more than five million endorsements, it will automatically be on The Vote. Then everyone starts to research the subject and to talk about it. It's really quite well done."

"I see." Thomas retrieved his drink and sat back next to Judith. "And whatever the majority decides today is then *the law* for at least the next year?"

"Yes," Ashley replied.

"On any subject? I mean, aren't there some issues that are just so obvious that they don't need to be voted on?"

"Maybe so. What was it, Ashley, eight years ago?" Dylan looked at his wife, for confirmation. "Yes, eight years ago we instituted this system to answer all of the confusion and garbage from one judge saying this, and another panel of judges saying that, and one legislature doing this, and Congress doing that. It was a huge mess. No one knew what was right and what was wrong, what was legal and what was illegal. Now the whole nation decides, every New Year's Eve, which laws to change, or leave unchanged, and then we all know exactly where we stand. No more confusion. No more gray areas. We're all governed by what the majority thinks is true and best."

"But aren't there some, I don't know, absolutes? Things, like, say, theft and murder, that don't need voting on?" Thomas asked.

"You Australians are obviously out of touch." Ashley smiled and passed the mixed nut tray. "Most of us in America have known for years that there are no absolutes. Everything is relative to each person's—or each society's—time and place. Long ago people used to say that America was founded on principles of absolute truths, but we know that America was really founded by men and women who just wanted to be free to create their own individual destinies. That's what we've designed The Vote to do. It lets us freely decide, as our society evolves, what is right and what is wrong, for us. For our time and place. It's a wonderful system."

There was a pause. "I see," Thomas finally said. "So what's on the ballot this year?"

Dylan put down his drink and picked up a folder from beside his chair on the floor. "I downloaded the voter's guide for today's Vote. It lists all the issues. Here's one. There's a proposal to raise the ceiling on legal theft from $250 to $500. Ashley and I don't like that one. We think $250 is plenty."

"You mean anyone in America can steal anything worth $250 or less, and it's legal?" Judith asked.

"Yes," Ashley replied. "We passed that a few years ago to help homeless people and to unclog the courts. The limit is per event. And of course, there can't be any violence associated with it. Just simple theft."

"You mean every day I can take $249 out of the cash register where I work and no one can complain?"

"Well, yes. But you wouldn't do that, Judith," Ashley said.

"Why wouldn't I?"

"Because you're a person who understands right and wrong. Like most of us."

"But you just said that you're voting on what's right and wrong, and if it's not wrong to take up to $250, why wouldn't I?"

"Because you just know that it's not right."

"But—"

Dylan turned to face the large screen interface. "Oh, they're starting. Ashley, is our terminal online and logged in?"

Ashley glanced at the steady green light on the small box to the left of the console. "We're on."

"Good. There'll be a brief introduction by the President, and then we'll start The Vote."

The President briefly praised the nation's annual opportunity for renewal and moving forward in the New Year. When she finished, the electronic voting began. Each issue was put on the screen for five minutes. Qualified voters could vote at any time. There was a fifteen-second warning that time was running out, and then The Vote was finished. All the results were given together at the end of The Vote, to encourage people to engage on all of the issues.

Ashley and Dylan each had a keypad connected wirelessly to the console. They turned in their chairs to face the large screen, and Dylan said, "OK, here we go."

The first issue came up: "In order to promote a better and healthier nation, The Birth Score should be raised from 105 to 110. Yes or No?"

"That's a tough one," Ashley said.

"What's The Birth Score?" Judith asked.

"Oh, it's the grading system they use to determine who is viable. There's one at birth and another one after any serious illness or injury if you're over age 65." Dylan answered.

"Viable?"

"Yes." Ashley turned to face her guests. "You know, they can do almost instant genetic testing now at birth, and even months before. Points are assigned for every imaginable trait of the fetus and the social condition of the parents, and if the minimum is not reached, then the baby is aborted or terminated."

"You mean the baby is killed? After it's born?" Judith asked.

"Not really. According to the law, they have one hour, but usually the genetic scan is completed and added to the social/economic score within ten minutes. So whether the fetus is terminated a few minutes before birth, or the 'baby' is terminated a few minutes after birth, it's the same. At most it's only 'alive' for a little while, and the result is much better for the rest of us."

"What sorts of things are scored?"

"Oh, you know, all of the genetic flags for diseases like cancer and hemophilia, heart murmur…the things you'd expect.

And then the parents are graded for income, intelligence, and those kinds of things. The points are added up, and if they don't reach 105, the fetus or baby is terminated. The Vote is asking whether to raise The Score to 110."

Judith shook her head silently.

Ashley smiled. "Hey, it's not bad. We're just helping Natural Selection with new technology. In fact, it's good. Remember how we had all of those unwed mothers giving birth thirty years ago, causing dysfunctional non-families? Now they assign negative 25 points to any unwed parent situation, so that baby has to be really special to pass. The result is far fewer teenage girls having babies. It's a huge improvement."

Thomas looked down at his drink. "I guess Jonathon would have been 'terminated' at birth."

Ashley looked at Thomas and frowned. "Oh, no. I don't think so. Dylan?"

"I don't know," her husband replied in a low voice.

Silence hung in the air.

Finally, Ashley said, "The time is almost up. I...I'm going to vote to leave it at 105." She pressed her keypad and a window on the screen registered that her "No" vote had been recorded.

"Me, too," Dylan added, and his vote was also recorded. "All right, does anyone else need a refill?" He stood.

"Yes, thanks," Thomas said, handing his glass to his host, his face still very serious.

The screen changed. "Here's an easier one," Ashley smiled. "The legal drinking age should be raised from 16 to 21. Yes or No."

"Sixteen?" Thomas asked.

"Crazy isn't it? That's the only problem with The Vote. Last year a lot of young people put a big block together to lower the age to 16, and I guess many folks just weren't looking or didn't vote, so it carried by a narrow margin. This year we're correcting it."

"For this past year sixteen year olds have been able to drink legally?"

"Yes. But not for much longer, we hope."

Thomas nodded. "I see. But going back to that last question, you said that you assign negative 25 birth points for the baby of an unwed mother. What are some other examples?"

"Well, they assign negative 10 points if one parent didn't finish high school, plus 15 if the parents are gay or from a minority, to correct for past discrimination, and negative 20 if one parent has a criminal record. Just normal stuff that you'd expect."

"You've got to be kidding," Judith almost whispered.

"Why?" Ashley answered. "It's actually pretty reasonable. We're just assisting Evolution to create the most productive people, while assuring that the best of the lower orders survive."

Thomas raised his hand. "Wait a minute. You're telling us that on the margin you 'terminate' more babies born to less educated parents because they are lower on the 'Evolutionary Order'?"

"Yes," Ashley nodded. "What's wrong with that?"

"I..." Thomas just shook his head.

"I mean," Ashley continued, "we know how important 'Diversity' is—celebrating how different we are. It only makes sense that if we are different, then some are better than others.

And that's exactly what Evolution says, too. So it all fits. And, again, it's not that we're killing anyone, for God's sake—unless you call a baby less than an hour old a 'person'—it's just that we're insuring through this point system that the best of the less desirables *do* survive, and then they are welcome in our society."

Glancing at each other, Judith and Thomas each took a sip from their glasses. Then Thomas moved forward on the couch. "Do I understand that with The Vote you could reinstate slavery, or decide that everyone over 90 ought to die, or anything you wanted?"

"Technically yes," Dylan answered, "but no one would ever vote for those things."

"Why not?"

Dylan smiled. "Because you just know that they're not right. I mean, it's obvious."

"It is? What if some scientific study showed that slavery is, on balance, best for society?"

"Don't be silly," Ashley said. "We know that slavery isn't right."

"How?"

"We just know. One person shouldn't enslave another. It's obvious." She stood and walked to the kitchen.

Thomas turned to Dylan. "But if right and wrong are not based on some absolute concepts, and are determined by a vote of the society, then why couldn't the society decide that slavery is a great idea? Or that children ought to be raised in state institutions, rather than by their parents? Or whatever?"

"Thomas, you exaggerate. We would never vote for things like that."

"How do you know?" Judith asked, slightly shaking her head.

Ashley, walking in from the kitchen, said, "People just know that those things wouldn't be right."

"How?"

"I don't know. They just know." She put a tray of cheese and crackers on the coffee table and sat down again.

Their Australian friends frowned. Thomas said, "Some of the things you've already told us seem pretty abhorrent to us, since we're from 'backward' Australia. If there's no truth except that everything is relative, and society decides truth on its own, then it seems to us that in fact *anything* is possible. And you seem to be proving that today."

"I wouldn't worry too much," Dylan said, picking up a cracker and adding a slice of cheese. "People are pretty reasonable and good. We don't think that there's much chance for abuse."

"But that's the thing. 'Abuse' is the wrong word, because it implies that you know right from wrong in the first place. With this system, right and wrong change every year. You can't 'abuse' anyone, because there is no standard to measure that term against. It's whatever you make it."

"We believe people are good at heart, so they know right from wrong inside."

Judith asked, "Really? Is that what Evolution and Natural Selection show us?"

"What do you mean?"

"How does Evolution create 'good' in someone's heart? Seems like only the strong and merciless would survive, not the 'good,' the one who might perish trying to help someone else."

Ashley laughed. "You're confusing me with all of this theory. I just know that The Vote is good, and it's working fine. We're evolving as a society without the hindrances of those supposed 'absolute truths' that some people used to talk about all the time. Honey, can you refresh my drink?"

Thomas sat forward. "They don't talk about absolute truth any more?"

Dylan stood. "We voted two years ago that since there are no absolute truths, no one can talk about them. Not in public, at least. We believe that people who try to fill our children with those sorts of thoughts are a detriment to our nation. Since Evolution and Relative Truth are proven facts, it's not fair to our children to cloud their minds with anything else.

"OK, honey," Dylan said, turning toward his wife. "We've got to vote on this one. Then there are, let's see, twenty-two more. Judith and Thomas, are you comfortable?"

Lie #5: There are no absolute truths. All truth is relative to the person and the situation.

Truth: God has created immutable physical laws by which the universe runs in a predictable manner. He has also created absolute truths for human behavior and revealed them to us in His Word, the Bible, and in the life of His son, Jesus Christ. These Truths do not change with circumstances; they are always true. When we do not follow them, we inevitably suffer negative consequences. These consequences may come immediately, or days, weeks or years later; but the negative consequences are just as true and predictable as is a chemical equation. Through His grace, God has also provided the way to restore our relationship with Him: belief in His son, who is that Way.

Beckwith, Francis J. and Gregory Koukl. *Relativism: Feet Firmly Planted in Mid-Air.* Grand Rapids, MI.: Baker Books, 1998.
Colossians 2:8
Romans 1:16-23
Bruce, Tammy. *The Death of Right and Wrong.* Roseville, CA.: Prima Publishing, a member of the Crown Publishing Group, a division of Random House, 2003.
John 18:33
http://www.cultural-relativism.com/
http://www.fRontiernet.net/~kenc/truth.htm
Copan, Paul. *True for You, But Not for Me.* Minneapolis: Bethany House Publishers, 1998.
Ephesians 6:13-18
2 Timothy 4:3-4
http://www.family.org/fofmag/cl/a0033123.cfm
Guinness, Os. *Time for Truth.* Grand Rapids, MI: Baker Books, 2000.
Veith, Jr., Gene Edward. *Postmodern Times.* Wheaton, IL.: Crossway Books, 1994.
http://www.str.org/free/commentaries/apologetics/index.htm#5relativism
http://www.geocities.com/mnapologetics/art3.htm

For the latest updates go to www.tenliesandtentruths.com

The Vote

Notes:

6

Leadership

Charlie Tate sat alone in his apartment near the university campus, the huge textbook open on the desk in front of him. He was tall, handsome and usually very much in charge. Except that right now, Charlie Tate couldn't believe his bad luck. He'd been accepted to the best business school in the country, but first he had to graduate with at least a 3.0 average. And tomorrow's Biology exam stood in the way.

This is so stupid! I don't need Biology for business. I should have studied more during the spring, but I hate all this science stuff.

Despite his many gifts and skills, science had never been a strength for him, and a bad final exam grade would undo all of his plans.

He turned the page to yet another diagram full of impossible names, took a sip of coffee, and tried to make sense of it. The phone rang next to him.

"Hey, Charlie, it's David." It was his roommate and best friend from before high school. "Charlie, I got it. The Biology final. Right here in my hand."

Charlie sat up. "What? Are you sure?"

"Yeah. The whole thing. Including the answers."

"No way."

"It's the real exam, the one Fletcher will give to your class tomorrow."

"How'd you get it?"

"Don't ask. Wanna see it?"

"Are you kidding?"

David mimicked the professor's squeaky voice. "I don't think that's quite right, Mr. Tate."

Charlie laughed. "It won't really be cheating, because I'll never need or use Biology. I just need this grade to get into business school."

"All right. I'm on the way."

Charlie put down the phone, jumped up and shouted. *Yes!*

****

Ten years later Charlie sat in his office at the corporate headquarters of Certified Solutions, a newly promoted senior project manager. Two proposals for packaging the company's latest software lay on the desk in front of him, and their company's lead designer, Preston, fifteen years Charlie's senior, sat across from him.

"The quality of the packaging is the same," said the designer, "but the Baker proposal is fifteen percent more expensive. We're going to need tens of thousands of these, so the total difference is huge."

Charlie looked carefully at the two proposals. "Preston, have we ever used Baker?"

"No. They're usually too expensive for what they provide. We can get the same or better quality from others at less cost. I think Baker may be getting a little soft. They've been in the business a long time, but I don't think Ralph Baker has invested in his company the way his dad did. Maybe a little too much golf." The designer ended with a smile.

"OK. I'll take a look at the proposals and let you know after lunch. Thanks for putting this together."

"No problem," said the other man as he rose to leave.

Three hours later, Charlie returned from a lunch meeting, took off his coat, and glanced at the framed photos of Karen and their two children, Meghan, 6 and Ryan, 3. He picked up the phone and punched the numbers he found in one of Preston's reports.

"Ralph Baker, please." A few moments later, the company's president was on the line.

"Mr. Baker, hey, this is Charlie Tate at Certified Systems. How are you?"

"Fine, Charlie. And, please, call me Ralph."

He swiveled in his chair and looked again at Baker's bio on their website. "Thanks. Listen, our designers have been looking at your proposal for our packaging requirement. Are you familiar with it?"

"Yes, of course. We'd certainly like to win that business. I personally approved the proposal. We cut the cost as much as we possibly could, while giving you the quality you need."

"Well, that's why I'm calling, Ralph. Are you sure you're as low as you can go? Excel is cheaper for the same quality."

"Charlie, they may say that now, but we hear they like to make substitutions when it's time for production."

Charlie shook his head. "We'd never allow it. Our two companies have never done much business, Ralph, which is a shame, being headquartered in the same city. Are you sure this is the best price you can give us?"

There was a pause. "If it will win the business, I'll take another five percent off. But that leaves us with almost no profit at all."

"Excel is fifteen percent less." He paused. Ralph did not respond.

"Ralph, aren't you on the Board of Trustees at Hightower School?"

"Uh, yes. A great school. Our family has supported it for years."

"It *is* a great school. My wife Karen and I are very impressed with it. And in fact, we hope that our daughter, Meghan, can start there next year in Kindergarten. She took their battery of tests but maybe didn't have her best day. She didn't feel well. Anyway, Karen and I certainly hope that she gets in."

There was another pause. "I see. Well, I'm sure that the school always wants a broad group of students. I imagine that they would be able to find a place for...Meghan, right?"

"Yes, Meghan. You really think so?"

"Oh, I'd be pretty certain."

Charlie smiled and swiveled again to look out the window. "Okay. That would make my two women very happy. And we'll keep considering this proposal from you on the packaging. I appreciate the five percent reduction. We'll spend a few days studying the quality issues and then get back to you."

"We'd really like to supply you on this one."

"I understand. Our lead designer will contact you in a couple of days."

"Fine. Thanks. Good-bye."

Charlie kept the receiver in his hand and dialed three digits.

"Preston, it's Charlie. I talked to Ralph Baker. He's going to take five percent off their bid, so I want to go with them—I know, but I like the quality of what they do, and he's local. We can absorb the extra cost somewhere else. Give Ralph a call this afternoon, if you can. And thanks again for all your help."

****

Ten years later Charlie was finishing a five-day business trip to London. With him in one of the finest restaurants in Kensington were his company's Director of Marketing, Stan Long, and two guests from the British company they were acquiring, Malcolm Griffiths, the Chairman, and Stephanie Bascombe, the Marketing Manager.

"Are you still pleased with your acquisition?" Griffiths, slightly overweight and balding, asked across the table, as the waiter departed with their orders.

Charlie raised his glass of whiskey as if to toast, and glanced to his left to look again into Stephanie's sparkling blue eyes. "By all means, Malcolm. Palisades is a great match for our new TransTech subsidiary. And we have been most impressed to learn how you've been marketing so successfully to European communications firms, haven't we Stan?" Charlie looked to his right.

"Yes, we certainly have," came the reply, as the three men acknowledged Stephanie.

A good eight years younger than her new boss, Stephanie Bascombe had been with them during the entire trip, and tonight Charlie thought she looked stunning in a burgundy dress with a high collar that nicely accented her curves. From their first meeting two months before in New York, Charlie had sensed an electricity between them, and the past five days had been like sublime torture, with the pressure mounting every time their eyes met and she smiled. Unmarried, Stephanie had suggested in many ways, Charlie thought, that he could expect more from his new European Marketing Director than just e-mails and memos.

"I hate to leave the business," Griffiths continued, "but we got a good price, and I know that I'm leaving our team in very capable hands."

Smiling, Charlie nodded his agreement as their second round of drinks arrived.

An hour later, after ordering their desserts, Charlie said, "Please excuse me for a minute. I need to find the facilities. Stan, could you join me, please?"

"Sure," Stan smiled, "sounds like a good idea, actually."

In the alcove leading to the restrooms, Charlie stopped and motioned Stan into a corner by the door.

"Listen, when dinner's over, I'm going to invite everyone to the bar, but I'd like you to say that we've got an early flight and you've got some work to catch up on. Okay?"

Stan smiled. "And you're hoping that Griffiths will need to get home to his wife, I assume."

Charlie nodded, a slight grin on his face. "Something like that. But even if he comes for one drink, I think I'll do just fine."

"I suspect so, too," Stan agreed, and gave his boss a knowing look.

"This isn't a regular thing. Karen and I are great. But we're thousands of miles from home, it's been a long and successful trip, and I think a little extra celebration for the CEO of a new multinational corporation might be in order."

Stan smirked knowingly. "You're the boss."

****

Ten years later Charlie was the CEO of MagnaCom, one of the largest telecommunications companies in the world, ringing the globe with fiber optic lines and supplying most large corporations and many governments with e-mail, voice and data connections. The original founder had handpicked him to take the reins of the company. Since coming onboard three years earlier, Charlie, through acquisitions and cost cutting, had increased revenues by more than three hundred percent, and profits by nearly that amount. His picture had been on the cover of every weekly magazine, looking wise with a head full of gray hair and a healthy tan. His pronouncements about business and the world economy were reported with great enthusiasm and respect. He had authored a best seller on effective management, and another was in the works.

He sat in his large corner office with the company's Chief Financial Officer on the fiftieth floor of their New York headquarters looking out at the Statue of Liberty. They were reviewing several summary reports and spreadsheets at Charlie's private conference table, in preparation for the company's upcoming quarterly report of earnings.

"We can't be that far off on our earnings projections, Stuart. The street will kill us," Charlie said, a clear note of anger and disbelief in his voice.

"I know. I know, Mr. Tate. It's those acquisitions in South America and the Middle East. They've just been slower to turn around than we expected."

Charlie studied the numbers and notes for several more minutes. *Meghan's getting married this month, and I've got to show Karen's new husband that I can pull off an incredible wedding. Then there's the beach house expansion. I need to exercise some options, and a drop in our stock price would be a disaster right now.*

"Can't we make some accounting elections that will get us through on paper for the next ninety days? Our South American business is rolling now, and the Middle East peace treaty should get us back on track there as well. Think of all the people who will be hurt if our stock price goes down because of this temporary situation."

Stuart half-nodded, and shrugged. "I don't know. I mean, I guess we could take some of those telecom operating expenses and capitalize them. That would decrease our expenses and increase our profit. In some cases with these new equipment categories it's a gray area, and our auditors might let us do a little of that."

Charlie smiled. "Now you're talking. Let's try to do a lot of that, and see how much we can get through. In fact, let's try to do enough to make a record quarterly profit...which we will, of course, once those two new markets kick in."

"I'm not sure," Stuart said. Noting the look on his boss's face, he quickly added, "But we'll certainly try."

"Good. And anything else you can do to help with this particular quarter's earnings will be greatly appreciated. Maybe to the tune of a significant bonus, Stuart."

The CFO smiled. "Thanks, Mr. Tate. Just doing my job."

"Exactly," Charlie smiled in response.

****

Eighteen months later, Charlie Tate was again in the national spotlight, this time appearing before a Senate sub-committee, which had subpoenaed him to explain the collapse of MagnaCom over a three week period, after it was disclosed that the company had been "cooking the books" to report fictitious profits for at least eight quarters. Charlie had resigned two weeks before and had tried to drop out of sight, but the public outcry over tens of thousands of lost jobs, imploded retirement plans, and ruined lives would not abate.

When Charlie had taken over at MagnaCom, many people had sensed that this would be the big one for him and had moved much of their life savings into MagnaCom stock. Among them were Stan, Stephanie, Ralph, Preston and David, each of whom knew about Charlie's effectiveness as a chief executive from personal experience. All had advised their friends to load up on MagnaCom stock, and they had then seen their savings completely wiped out. When their friends asked them about the allegations of fraudulent stock manipulation, each of his five old friends said, "I just don't understand what happened. I've known Charlie for years, and I can't believe that he would ever do anything like that."

All except Karen, his former wife, who shorted 10,000 MagnaCom shares on the first rumors of problems with the company, and pocketed a small fortune.

Lie #6: Character doesn't count. Only results do.

Truth: Character is the basis for everything that one does. Without good character based on God's Truths, people break laws that God has set for our behavior, inevitably leading to the negative consequences described above.

Job 4:8
Proverbs 11:18
Hosea 10: 12-13
Proverbs 22:8
Galatians 6: 7-9
Nehemiah 1:11
Matthew 25:14-30
http://www.vanguard.com/bogle_site/sp20020410.html
http://www.bluinc.com/news/character.html
http://www.crosswalk.com/faith/ministry_articles/guestcolumns/1
        108776.html

For the latest updates go to www.tenliesandtentruths.com

Notes:

Ten Lies and Ten Truths

7

Definitions

Ryan Harding returned to his spacious office on the fifth floor of the company's suburban headquarters, nestled into a secluded campus-like setting. The leaves were almost gone from the trees outside his window, and the temperature had been dropping throughout the afternoon as a cold front moved in.

He sat in his chair, picked up the phone, and turned to face the picture on his desk as he dialed home.

"Hey, it's me. How's your day been? Good... Yes, very cold. We'll need the new blanket tonight. Listen, I've got to meet someone from the office right after work. Tom Redmond....I don't know. He didn't say. He's in Sales....Yes, very nice. Our age....I don't know....Just said he wanted to talk to me away from the office. It happens sometimes in HR....We'll see. I just wanted to let you know. I won't be late. Home for dinner....Yes. OK?....I love you, too."

He swiveled back to his computer to check e-mails and voicemails, then his schedule. His small Human Resources Department stayed busy meeting the needs of their sometimes struggling company, but Ryan's two decades of experience and his can-do staff made it possible to stay just ahead of the curve. He had three meetings that afternoon on middle management training, next year's budget, and evaluating their psychological testing program. And then an unexpected appointment with Tom Redmond in the bar at a nearby restaurant.

It was almost dark as he pulled into the parking lot and walked towards the tastefully lit, upscale Da Vinci restaurant, hugging his overcoat around him in the brisk wind. In a row of booths along the side wall of the quiet bar, he spotted Tom Redmond, who smiled and waved him over.

Tom stood and extended his hand as Ryan approached.

"Ryan, thank you for coming. Please have a seat, and what are you drinking?"

Ryan nodded. "Scotch and water sounds good on a night like this. Thanks."

While Tom went to the bar to place the order, Ryan removed his overcoat and slid into the booth.

Tom returned. "The best they've got. Water on the side."

Ryan smiled and accepted the two glasses from one of the senior executives in their company's Sales Division, who slid into the booth across from him.

"Thanks, Tom. Pat and I have dinner here often. Good food." Ryan tipped his glass toward Tom and took a sip. He smiled again and waited.

Tom cleared his throat. "Thanks again for coming. I have something I want to talk with you about, and I just didn't feel comfortable mentioning it in the office. I, uh, thought I'd like to get your sort of informal opinion and advice."

Tom looked down briefly at his glass, took another good swig, and returned it to the table. Finally, he looked up at his guest.

"First, I want you to know how much I respect you and Pat for coming out. I mean, I know it took some courage in your position to let the rest of the company know you're gay, and, personally, I think it's terrific. From the times I've met Pat, I think he's a great guy, and all of us, except maybe the usual few bigots, are proud of both of you."

"Thank you," Ryan nodded slightly again and smiled. "It wasn't easy at first, but the support of so many in the company has been great. We feel very loved and accepted."

"That's right. And I heard that you got married?"

Ryan straightened up and his smile broadened. "Yes, three weeks ago. As soon as the Supreme Court ruled it was unconstitutional to deny gay marriages. We were married on that next Saturday afternoon with several old friends who came for the wedding. We had a quick one night 'honeymoon,' but we're going on our real honeymoon cruise over Christmas. We're committed to each other."

Tom took another sip and nodded. "And with your official marriage, Pat now gets your benefits, right?"

Ryan nodded. "Yes. That's important for us. He's now covered by our company medical and dental policies, and by our life insurance."

Tom looked down. "I'm very glad for you and Pat." He studied his drink.

Ryan prompted him. "So, Tom, how are you? What did you want to talk about?"

Tom took a sip. "Well, it's kind of like your situation, Ryan. I need your advice and help."

Ryan leaned forward. "How can I help? You're not gay, are you?"

Tom shook his head. "No. But I guess I kind of wish I were. You guys have really made great progress. You've got it together."

"Then, what is it?"

"Well, Ryan...I have three wives."

Ryan leaned back slowly. "Three wives?"

"Yes. But it's not what you think. We all live together very happily. And we have six children."

"Three wives and six children." Ryan stroked his chin thoughtfully.

Tom continued. "Yes. We're all *very* happy. We think it's perfectly normal and natural. It's a long story, how it happened. But we feel that God wants us to be together. Like it's the right thing. Like it's how God created us."

"*Everyone* is happy?"

"Well, there is some infighting among the kids, especially the boys. We think that's true in all families, you know?"

"Yes, I guess so."

"So, here's the thing. I'm really only legally married to Maria, at least in this state. We went out of state for the other two weddings and just didn't divulge all the details on the wedding licenses. You know?" He smiled again and took another sip, watching Ryan's eyes.

Ryan nodded again.

"We're tired of living in the shadows. We want to come out and tell the world about our love for each other, just as you've done."

"I see."

"Now that the Supreme Court has said that marriage is not just between one man and one woman, we want to be officially married, too."

"I guess I never thought about it."

"It makes sense, doesn't it?"

Ryan turned his glass on its wooden coaster and thought for a moment.

"I guess...I don't know. Would there be any limit to the number of wives?"

"Why? If marriage is basically whatever consenting adults want it to be, then why should the government place any restrictions on it?"

"Uh, I never thought about it that way."

Tom leaned forward. "And here's the really important part. We want and need those benefits. We deserve them."

As Ryan looked off into the distance, Tom continued. "We have huge expenses every month with the kids, but only the two I had with Maria are covered by our company's benefit package. I'm scared that two of the others may have serious problems that will need long term medication, maybe operations. We live in fear that one of the kids will fall, or get hurt on a bike. Not to mention my other two wives, Julia and Teri. We need those benefits, Ryan."

Ryan pressed his back against the leather of the booth. "Company benefits?"

"Yes, of course. Just like you and Pat."

"Well, but Tom, covering so many dependents just doesn't seem feasible. I mean, our plan isn't set up for that."

"I know." His voice rose a bit and he leaned further forward. "But that's just the point. The plan wasn't set up for covering Pat until marriage was redefined. And now it covers him. We want the same thing. It's only right. It's only fair."

"I, uh....I hadn't thought about it."

"Well, it's the right thing to do. You gays had marriage redefined to fit how you feel, and now we want marriage redefined to fit how we feel."

Ryan took another sip. "But what if someone has ten wives—or husbands, I guess—and twenty kids? Our company's benefit plan would go bankrupt before it could pay for all of them."

Tom leaned in further, a note of anger creeping into his voice. "You of all people should understand our problem. Somehow the company found the money in the budget to add Pat—and all the other recent gay marriage partners. Why not *my* family?"

"I...do you think that your kind of marriage—I guess it's polygamy—will be approved in the courts anytime soon?"

Tom smiled. "Yes. Thanks largely to what you've done, we feel confident that our form of marriage will be approved very soon. Given what the courts said about traditional marriage, that it's no longer the 'only' way, how could anyone argue against us?"

"I guess you're right."

"Exactly. And here's the thing, Ryan. There are at least five families like ours in the company. We kind of hope that you, through your national HR connections, will become a champion for our rights with other corporations, just like the gay community united in the 90s. We'd like you to get out in front, to set an example for tolerance and acceptance of our marriage style. Hopefully other companies will follow our company's example."

Ryan took a deep breath, and said with a smile that was more a grimace, "Really?"

"Having just recently gained your own rights, we believe you're the perfect person to lead this movement. Sort of an Alliance for Justice. What do you think?"

"Uh...Can I look at the math, first, to see what effect it will have on the rest of us?"

Tom became more animated. "The math? Ryan, this is a principle! If marriage is right for you and Pat, then it has to be right for Maria, Teri, Julia and me! The principle of equal justice is all that's important here. Why would you have to do any math?"

Ryan pursed his lips and raised his hands. "Okay. You're right. I'll help."

Tom smiled, nodding his head. "There's one more thing."

Ryan drained his glass. "What's that?"

Tom dropped his voice. "If you help us win this one, think about it. You say that you and Pat are in a 'committed relationship.' But if you help us get our kind of marriage declared constitutionally protected, gay polygamy will follow immediately."

Ryan sat silently, mulling it over. Only this time he wasn't frowning.

Tom continued. "Think about it. If gay marriage is okay, and polygamy is okay, then gay polygamy should also be okay."

"You mean Pat and me and several other guys, all legally married?"

Tom nodded. "Yes."

Ryan sat back in the booth. "Wow."

Lie #7: Marriage must be redefined.

Truth: Marriage is ordained by God to be between one man and one woman. The traditional family is the first and foundational building block of all societies, preceding the church and state. If children result, they will be nurtured and raised by committed parents who use and pass on the strengths, talents, and resources of both individuals and both genders. If marriage is ever redefined to be anything other than one man and one woman, then it can be stretched to include anything and everything, and therefore mean nothing.

http://www.weeklystandard.com/Content/Public/Articles/000/000/
   002/938xpsxy.asp?pg=1
http://www.christiantimes.com/Articles/Articles%20Jul04/Art_Jul0
   4_oped1.html
Genesis 2:20-25
Matthew 19:4-6
http://www.ftlcomm.com/ensign/editorials/LTE/thornton/thornton
   list/thornton097/gayMarriage.html
http://www.townhall.com/columnists/maggiegallagher/mg2004031
   6.shtml

For the latest updates go to www.tenliesandtentruths.com

Notes:

Ten Lies and Ten Truths

8

The Game Show

The floor manager raised his clipboard just out of camera range and motioned to the four well-dressed people standing in the bright lights on the multi-colored game show set.

"We're on in…three, two, one…"

As he brought down his clipboard, the fiftyish host on the left side of the stage engaged his smile, focusing on Camera One.

"Hello and welcome to *Truth Pursuit*, the high powered game show where we focus on the truth, not trivia. I'm your host, Rob Palmer, and we invite you to join us for the next thirty minutes as we seek to separate truth from fiction."

The audience applauded on cue. Palmer, still smiling, turned to face the three contestants. Each stood behind individual consoles to the right of the large, vertical game board that occupied the middle of the stage.

"As you know, once a month we play our special *Celebrity Truth Pursuit* game. Today we've invited three well-known personalities, and each has designated a charity to which his or her winnings will be donated. Please help me welcome our guests."

A camera focused on the panelist closest to the game board. Palmer voiced over her image. "From America's news capital, please welcome Ms. Patricia Keenan, senior editor of the nation's most prestigious newspaper, *The National Times*."

While the audience applauded, Ms. Keenan, in her late forties and dressed in a blue suit with a vibrant red scarf, smiled and nodded.

As the camera moved to the right, Palmer continued, "In the middle position, please say hello to Mr. Tyrone Lewis, founder of the well known 'Association of Collegiate Educators.' We're glad you're here, Mr. Lewis."

More applause. With a smile and a wave of the hand the impeccably dressed, rather thin African-American with gold rimmed glasses and a dark blue handkerchief jutting from his suit pocket acknowledged the audience.

"Finally, a man who needs no introduction to television viewers. Please give a big *Truth Pursuit* welcome to the anchor on Cable News Group's Evening News, Mr. Brad Woods."

The applause intensified as Woods, youthful and tan despite his obvious years, nodded to the game show host and then smiled into the camera.

Another camera cut in for a close-up of Rob Palmer. "All right, we'll learn a little more about each celebrity guest and the charity that he or she has designated as the game goes on, but right now let's start with our first question."

Palmer turned to face the contestants and the camera pulled back to show the entire stage. On the large game board in the center, twenty-five squares were arranged in a five by five grid. Above each of the five vertical columns was a subject header.

"All right, contestants. The object is to spell the word TRUTH from left to right, mixing any rows to accomplish it. There are five categories of questions, and today we've chosen questions centered on current events, politics, and American history. We hope to give away a lot of money to the charities you've chosen. The questions on the bottom row are worth $500 each, and on the top row, $5,000. The harder the question you answer, the more money you win for your charity. The person who puts the last letter in TRUTH wins that letter plus an additional $5,000. At the end, we have our super round, when all of the amounts are doubled. Once I've asked the question and given the three possible answers, only one of which is true, as soon as you think you know it, touch your buzzer. If you fail to get the right answer, either of the other two panelists can ring in and try. All right, if we're ready, let's begin. Patricia, we'll let you select the first question."

The newspaper editor smiled and nodded. "Thank you, Rob. Let's try *Family Economics* for $3,000."

The square exactly in the center of the game board lit up.

"Great, Patricia. Here's the question. In America today, what percentage of African-American families are at or below the poverty level, when both parents are present? Is it

A. 25%

B. 15%, or

C. 8%?"

The console in front of Tyrone Lewis immediately lit up as he hit his buzzer. The camera shifted to him. "That's easy, Rob. It's at least 25%."

A gong sounded. Lewis frowned. The camera shifted back to the whole group.

"No, Tyrone, I'm…"

Patricia's console lit up. "It must be 15%."

The gong again.

Palmer shook his head again. "No, I'm sorry, Patricia." He looked at the card in his hand. "When husband and wife stay together, the incidence of poverty in African-American homes is only 8%. It's even lower if they both work. But in single parent homes, the incidence is five times higher, at 40%.

"I'm sorry that no one got the first question, but that leaves the full board to spell on. Brad, it's your turn to choose a category and a dollar amount."

The evening news anchor smiled, shifted on his feet and said, "All right, Rob, let's try *American History* for $4,000."

The next to the top square in the first column lit up. "Okay, if any of you gets this one, we'll have the first T in TRUTH, and one of you will have $4,000 for your charity. Here's the question. On the day that the House of Representatives passed the First Amendment to the U. S. Constitution, commonly referred to as erecting the Wall of Separation between Church and State, the same legislators also passed:

A. A bill expressing its official displeasure with the Catholic Church for trying to influence the vote in local elections in New England;

B. A bill asking President Washington to set aside a day of prayer and fasting to thank God for the new Constitution; or

C. A bill funding the teaching of religion and morality in public schools in the newly formed territories to the west."

There was a pause. Finally, Brad Woods hit his buzzer. Palmer nodded.

"Well, it doesn't seem like either of the last two would be right, given the Separation of Church and State, so I guess I'll go with the first one."

The gong. The contestants looked at each other. Patricia Keenan shrugged and touched her buzzer. "Rob, I guess they might have thought that religion would make some sort of general moral difference, so they probably approved spending money on that, and I'll pick C."

The gong again.

"I'm sorry, Patricia. Congress did pay for teaching religion in the schools, but it was done six weeks *before* passing the First Amendment. On the same day in September, 1789, when the House of Representatives passed the First Amendment, those same members called on the President to thank God for so clearly helping in the difficult task of creating the Constitution, a document which at that time was unique in all the world."

He was about to continue when Brad Woods interrupted. "Are you sure of that? We know that there's a separation of Church and State in our country. How could the same representatives vote for separation but also explicitly thank God for the Constitution? That can't be right."

Palmer shrugged and looked down at his cards. "I understand. But all of our questions are reviewed by a panel of experts. It says in my notes that the date was September 25, 1789."

"Then why call it a 'Wall of Separation' if the first Congress was paying for religious teaching in the schools and openly thanking God for the Constitution?" Woods asked.

Palmer smiled. "I don't know. Well, anyway, I'm sorry that we've stumped you with the first two questions. But let's take a quick break, and after the commercial, Patricia, please tell us about the charity you've selected."

*****

Following the break Rob Palmer addressed the newspaper editor.

"So, Patricia, tell us about the charity that you've designated for your winnings today."

"For twenty years I've been supporting the We Want Babies Foundation. The foundation helps insure that babies are born only when the mother really wants them and is ready to love and care for them."

"And how do you do that, Patricia? Through adoption?" Palmer asked.

"We insure that every baby is wanted through guaranteeing the mother's right to choose."

"Thank you, and, again, good luck. Let's move on with our next question. Tyrone, it's your turn to choose."

"I think it's time to get some points on the board. Let's try a low value one. How about *Science* for $500?"

The bottom right square lit. Palmer said, "Okay, if you get this, it will be the H in TRUTH. Here's the question. Darwin postulated in the 1850's that his theory of evolution would be proven correct because all lower life forms would be shown to be very simple, as he predicted, and that as one moved up the evolutionary scale, life forms would become much more complex. Recently scientists have found that the bacteria flagellum, a tiny "rotary motor" spinning at 17,000 rpm, is used to propel bacteria in liquids and:

> A. Is incredibly simple in its structure, showing
>   scientists how it could easily mutate into the higher
>   forms that Darwin predicted on the evolutionary ladder.

B. Is moderately complex but still simple in basic structure, showing that the flagellum has itself evolved over the ages.

C. Is incredibly complex, with over forty essential parts which were invisible to Darwin, each of which interlocks in ways that imply a simultaneous origin, because their functions are totally dependent on each other."

Lewis pounded his buzzer. "It must be one of the first two, and I think you're being a little sneaky today, so I'll choose B."

Gong. Lewis frowned.

Patricia Keenan quickly hit hers. "A. It has to be A."

Gong again. Keenan scowled at Palmer.

"I'm sorry again panel. Apparently, the truth is that these forms, which Darwin thought to be the most simple building blocks for more complex forms, are actually also incredibly complex. And that's just as true of the ones preserved from long ago, as it is for ones living today. They're the same." He looked up and saw the glares from the panel. "I know. But it's on the card."

Lewis started to speak but Palmer continued quickly. "And now it's time for another break."

****

When the show returned after the commercials, calm seemed to have been restored, and everyone was smiling.

"Before we take our next question, Tyrone, please tell us about the charity which you hope to help today."

"Certainly, Rob. It's funny that you'd have a question on Darwin, because I'm supporting the Black is Best Foundation. This group has done research to disprove Darwin, and to show that the original, purest forms of human life were our Black ancestors in Africa. And that everyone else since then are much less pure and much less capable."

"Interesting. Interesting. Thank you. All right, panel, let's hope that you start to rack up the money for your charities with this next question. Patricia, it's your turn again to choose the question."

"Okay. Let's try *Science* again for $1,000."

The square above the previous one in the lower right corner lit.

"Here's your question. In 1973, the prestigious American Psychiatric Association reclassified homosexuality from a disorder, like polygamy or incest, into normal behavior. This change was the result of the following scientific studies in the preceding ten years:

> A. A study of cadavers showing that homosexuality is directly related to the size of the anterior hypothalamus in the human brain.
>
> B. An exhaustive experiment with over 5,000 homosexuals showing that in all other activities and relationships their characteristics were well within the bounds of "normal."
>
> C. There were no scientific studies as the basis for this change."

Patricia hit her buzzer. "It's obviously answer B, Rob."

Gong.

Woods touched his buzzer. "Then it must be A. In fact, I think we reported on that study a couple of years ago."

Gong.

"What?" Woods asked.

"I'm sorry, panel. The truth is that the reclassification occurred only because the gay lobby violently disrupted the meetings of the APA for four years and threatened its governing Board until they agreed to change the designation. And it says on my card here, Brad, that the study you reported on has been discredited because its procedure has never been able to be repeated by any other researcher. All right, we have to move on. Time is running short. Brad, can you quickly tell us about your charity?"

"Well, it's sort of like Tyrone and the question on Darwin. I happen to be supporting the Gay Boy Guides. This is a new organization for boys, so that those of us who are enlightened and realize that there really is no difference can send our sons off camping with openly gay older teenagers and male leaders. It's an idea whose time has come."

"And how is the Gay Boy Guides idea catching on?"

"To date it's been a little slow, but it's new. And that's why I'm supporting it."

"Great. Well, now that we've heard about all three charities, let's try to get them some money today. So far, we aren't doing as well as we hoped, but there are still a couple of questions remaining. Brad, it's your turn again."

"Let's try *International Policy* for $1,000."

"Here's your question, panel. A 1972 report with global recommendations published by a group known as the Club of Rome has been called a huge mistake. One recent critic charged that if the report had been adopted, 'people the world over would have suffered immensely and would have been condemned to perpetual poverty with little hope of improving their lives.' The Club of Rome was:

> A. A group of wealthy industrialists who recommended more trade, less government spending on social welfare, and fewer taxes across the globe.
>
> B. A panel of prestigious scientists who, using an MIT computer model, predicted limits on world growth from the depletion of natural resources like oil and food.
>
> C. A pro-life action committee that called for more live births and increasing populations in all nations."

Lewis' buzzer sounded. "Clearly the answer is C. With unbridled population growth, there must be destitute poverty."

Gong.

"No way," Lewis said.

Keenan's buzzer went off. "Then it must be A. With less government spending on social welfare, people would have little hope for improvement in their lives."

Gong.

"It must be," Lewis repeated.

Palmer looked intently at his cards. "The answer is B. The Club of Rome was a group of imminent international scientists who met in the late 1960s. They published *Limits to Growth* in 1972, which received wide publicity in the press. In it, they predicted that by 2000, the world would run out of farm land, food, oil, copper, silver, etc., and that world health would be undermined by exponential increases in population and pollution. They called for strict government controls as the world's only hope. But in fact, without adopting any of their recommendations, none of their predictions has proven to be true. With few exceptions across the globe, people live longer, eat more, and have rising incomes, declining pollution, and lower food prices than in 1972."

"Hmpf," Lewis said, frowning.

Palmer tried to smile at his guest. "I'm sorry. Those are the facts. Unfortunately, we still have no part of TRUTH spelled and no income on the board for your charities, and we're down to our last question. So this is the super round, and any winnings will be doubled. Tyrone it's your turn."

"All right. I don't like how this has gone so far. Let's try *Family Economics* one last time for $4,000."

"I'm just as sorry as you are," Palmer said, as he pulled up the question card. "Here is our last question. If the federal income tax rate for the upper 60% of income earners was reduced by ten percent, what would be the effect on the lower 40% of income earners?

> A. Their immediate share of the nation's income tax burden would increase.
> B. There would be no effect.
> C. Their long term tax burden would increase because of interest on the increased debt created by the resulting deficits.

No buzzer sounded. The contestants looked at each other.

Finally, Keenan hit hers. "I think we're all a little gun shy. But let me take a crack at it. When we started, I would have jumped at A as being the most logical, or perhaps C. But based on what we've learned in the last thirty minutes, I'm going to guess

B, which seems illogical, but may be correct. I couldn't tell you why."

For the first time that day a series of pleasant chimes sounded.

"Yes, Patricia, you're right!" Palmer exclaimed. "B is the correct answer. There would be no effect on the lower 40% of income earners of reducing taxes on everyone else."

Keenan shook her head. "I'm glad to win, but why, Rob?"

He smiled. "It says on the card because the lower 40% of income earners in America pay no Federal income tax. Any change in the tax rate to the rest of us won't alter the proportion they pay, since they pay no tax anyway. And in every recent example of a tax rate reduction, tax receipts have actually increased, so no long term deficit was created by a tax cut."

No one on the panel said anything.

Palmer smiled and continued. "Well, we're out of time. This is the first time I can remember that we only got a single answer right. I'm sorry that there weren't more. But we wish you and your charities all the best."

He turned to face the audience. The camera pulled in tight. "Until next time, please keep up the Pursuit of Truth!"

The Game Show

Lie #8: The Elites know better than you how to raise families and govern the nation.

Truth: Experts are always important for specific knowledge and expertise. God wants us to gain knowledge and to be the best possible stewards of the world He created. But knowledge is not wisdom. And knowledge is not always Truth. Judgment, wisdom, values, and morality are foundational to families and to nations. These truths are passed from generation to generation by faith, family and friends. Always seek input from trusted experts. But also seek truth, wisdom and judgment from God and those whom He places closest to you.

Maher, Bridget, Editor. *The Family Portrait.* Washington, D.C.: Family Research Council, 2002.
Sowell, Thomas. *The Vision of the Anointed: Self-Congratulation as Basis for Social Policy.* New York: Basic Books, a member of the Perseus Books Group, 1995.
1 Corinthians 1:20-31
2 Timothy 3:14-17

Poverty
http://www.smartmarriages.com/lATimes.html
http://www.census.gov/hhes/poverty/histpov/hstpov4.html
http://www.census.gov/population/www/socdemo/race/black.html

Exercise of Belief in God
http://www.reclaimamerica.org/PAGES/NEWS/newspage.asp?story=1294
http://www.achw.org/sepcs.htm

Flagellum
http://ourworld.compuserve.com/homepages/rossuk/Behe.htm
http://www.millerandlevine.com/km/evol/design1/article.html

Hypothalamus
http://www.adherents.com/misc/glbt_science.html

Club of Rome
http://www.foreignpolicy.com/Ning/archive/archive/133/dustbin.pdf

http://www.overpopulation.com/faq/natural_resources/limits_to_g
  rowth.html

Tax Cuts
http://www.nationalreview.com/balance/balance081701.shtml

For the latest updates go to www.tenliesandtentruths.com

Notes:

Ten Lies and Ten Truths

9

The Past is Present

Justin Woods had spent Tuesday night with his friend Paul Strickland. School was out the following day, due to a teacher conference. The two boys had slept late, not hearing Paul's dad leave for work.

Paul, the only child of a recently divorced couple, was used to spending time on his own. He had persuaded his father to let Justin spend the night so that the boys could study together for their mid-term exams, which were coming up the following week.

But studying was not on their agenda that Wednesday morning. Maybe later. Instead, they rummaged through the large assortment of adult movies that Paul had discovered in a file drawer of his dad's study. The drawer had been locked until Paul found the key in the back of his dad's desk while searching for change the week before.

After reviewing the titles of the treasure trove he'd discovered, Paul knew that he had to share them with Justin. So they had carefully orchestrated the sleepover on a day when they knew that they wouldn't be disturbed.

"If some are not rewound, we need to be sure to put them back exactly where we start," Paul said.

"Okay, so we'll set the counter to 0 on each one as we start it, and then we can return to that exact place," Justin agreed.

As they looked through the titles and the covers, their eyes almost popped out of their heads.

"Wow," Justin exclaimed. "Where did your Dad get all of these?"

"I don't know." Paul shook his head. "I remember one night when he and Mom were yelling at each other, I heard her say something about Dad living in a fantasy world of his movies. I thought she meant movies at the theater—but he doesn't go to them much."

Justin smiled. "I guess you understand now."

"Yeah, these are awesome."

"Like, incredible."

"I wonder if he watches them with Suzie." Suzie had been his father's secretary. Paul learned during the divorce that his Dad had begun an affair with the much younger woman a year before his parents broke up. He wasn't sure about their current relationship. Sometimes Suzie spent the night at his Dad's house; sometimes someone else did. At least Paul suspected that it happened from the articles of clothing left around, and from the scheduling challenges of his parents.

Paul turned on the player and Justin carefully inserted the first movie. He then pressed PLAY, and up came "A Hard Dazed Night." The boys were instantly transported to a fantasy world that they could never have imagined on their own at age thirteen. The images on the large screen soon sent their systems into overload.

When the movie finished, Justin touched rewind and looked at Paul. Both of them were still considering what they had just seen. "I wonder if all adults have these kinds of movies," Justin said.

"I don't know. What's the point if you're married?" Paul asked.

"Yeah. I'm pretty sure my folks don't," Justin said. "I can't see them with these." He held up two of the packages. He couldn't explain it, but he was relieved to be able to say that. Then he looked again at their choices for the day, as the first movie completed its rewinding. He was glad that Paul's dad had no such scruples.

When the second movie was over, the boys took a break to fix sandwiches. Sitting at the breakfast room table, Justin said, "Maybe we ought to study some."

"Are you kidding? We can *always* study. These movies are incredible."

Back in the den, Justin started "House Party III," and they settled back into the recliners in front of the large screen.

Ten minutes into the movie, a young brunette joined the fun, and Justin's eyes squinted to take a closer look. She looked vaguely familiar. While he was studying the young woman, Paul suddenly said, "Hey, Justin, that girl looks just like your mom!"

Justin was speechless. His mom was, what…thirty-two? And still very good looking, all his friends said. When the young woman on the screen spoke, Justin was sure that it was either his Mom or someone who looked exactly like her. Naked. With….

He jumped up. "We gotta stop this!" he said, and pushed STOP on the player. It went dark. He looked down at the tape cover. "House Party III" it said, and one of the women pictured around the patio pool could definitely have been a younger version of his mother. The name next to her was Linda Lee.

He shook his head. "Gross." Then he turned to look at Paul, who was still sitting in the recliner, and tossed him the box.

Paul said, "It must be a mistake. Linda Lee is not her name. It must be someone who looks like her."

"I don't know."

"Want to try another one?"

Justin shook his head. "No. I think I better just go home."

Paul stood up. "Yeah. OK. I'll put all of this away."

"Sorry. That was just too weird."

Justin trudged back to Paul's room, gathered his stuff and rode his bike the three blocks to his home.

Could that really have been my mom? With all those men...and women? Gross! It must be a mistake.

****

Two weeks went by. When he was not at school or studying, Justin racked his brain trying to figure out how to broach the subject of the movie with his mother. He couldn't shake the visual images in the movie. And her voice, his *mother's* voice, in a porn movie. It had to be a mistake. They lived in a pleasant, middle class suburb of St. Louis. His dad was an accountant, and his mom worked thirty hours a week as an executive assistant in a real estate office. They attended church regularly. Justin was an only child and had always been close to his mom, who, now that he thought about it, was younger than the parents of most of his friends.

The mid-term exams were a blur, and Justin knew that he hadn't hit his usual high marks. Ironically, the arrival of his mid-term report gave him the opportunity he had been agonizing over. On Saturday morning his father had gone to the hardware store to buy leaf bags, and his mom had walked out to the mailbox to get the mail, dressed in a baggy sweatshirt and jogging pants, with a mug of coffee in her hand. When she returned, she opened the report from the school, and then called to Justin, who was in his room.

"Justin, can you come down here, please?"

Without answering, he pounded down the stairs, his arms and legs a thirteen-year-old jumble. When he reached the bottom of the stairs, he saw the open envelope in his Mom's hand, and looked down.

"What happened to your grades?"

He shook his head. "I don't know. I guess I didn't do well."

"But you always do so well in math and science. You barely passed the exams this time. Honey, is something wrong?"

He glanced up at her. She had that mixture of concern, confusion and disappointment that always made him feel bad when he let her down. He lowered his eyes, felt a chill, and whispered, "House Party III."

She took a step towards him. "What did you say?"

He looked up and into her eyes. "House Party III," he repeated.

Her eyes and mouth opened, then her eyes narrowed again as she seemed to be processing what he had said.

"What does that mean?" she said, but he could tell that she knew.

"I watched House Party III—or the first part of it. Was that...?" He looked down again. "Was that you?"

"Oh, Justin." Her body seemed to go limp. She put down the coffee mug and walked over to him. She stretched out her arm to hug him but he backed away.

"It *was* you! With those guys!" He took another step back. "Gross! Paul, and I guess now all his friends, have seen *you* in that movie."

His mom inhaled and shook her head. She said nothing. The two of them just looked at each other. Finally, she said, "We've got to talk. Here, come sit at the table."

He didn't say anything but followed her into the kitchen, where she poured more coffee and then joined him in their breakfast nook. They had a round table next to a bay window that looked out on their garden. The back yard was filled with late morning fall sunshine. Justin and his mom sat so that they could both see out the bay window, with one chair between them.

Justin looked down at his hands, and his mom studied her coffee. He looked up, and she seemed to be deep in thought. Finally she took a sip, put down the mug, and, still looking at it, said, "I've dreaded this day for years and years, Justin. I hoped it would never come, and especially with you being thirteen." She looked at him, and he returned her gaze. "I won't even ask how you and Paul came to see the movie at your age, because I guess it's not important, really." She stopped, took another deep breath, and Justin could see a tear running unchecked down her right cheek. "It *was* me in that movie. And in three others."

Justin grimaced.

"I was young and stupid. All through high school people told me how beautiful I was, and I was serious about acting. My parents didn't have much money, so when I graduated I decided that rather than going into debt for college, I would move to California, get a job as a waitress or something, and try to break into movies." She sighed. "It's a long story, but eventually the agency fees took all my money. A guy I'd met told me that he thought I could do well in adult movies, and I ought to try them."

She paused and looked at her son. "I didn't have my faith then. My generation had grown up on the tail end of 'If it feels good, do it.' I was alone. Others were doing it and making some money. I figured that it would be like waitressing—I'd just do it for a while to support myself, before making it in real movies."

She closed her eyes and shook her head, then opened them again and said, "It *was* 'gross' at first. It didn't seem right. But I was doing it, and everyone else was doing it, and they paid us a lot of money. All those men who buy videos or pay for movies in hotels don't realize that all of those dollars make it possible for the movie producers to hire lots of new young girls like I was, right off the street. I got caught up in it."

Finally Justin said something. "But Mom, it's so gross."

She looked intently at her son and nodded. "I know. I know. It's not what God wants. It's terrible. But it's like many awful things. You know deep inside that it's wrong, but then there's some short term reason—money, pleasure, ego, something—that keeps you doing it. It's like it has a power over you.

"I'm sorry that I did it, and I'm very sorry that I hurt you. I've dreaded this day. I hoped you'd never find out. That's the thing about these movies. Once you've been in one, you can never take it back. It's always out there, somewhere, for a child or parent or spouse to see. It never goes away. It just eats at me."

"Why did you stop?"

She smiled for the first time. "Because I had you."

"What?"

She took a deep breath and then a sip of coffee. She looked out the bay window for a moment, and then back at her son. "I got pregnant somewhere around the time of the third or fourth movie. I—I'm not even sure by whom. Anyway, I now think that God used my getting pregnant to change me. They wanted me to have an abortion, but I wouldn't. Over about a week of thinking and, I guess, praying, I woke up and realized what I was doing. It wasn't that I suddenly 'got religion.' It was just that I knew that what I'd been doing was wrong, and that I had to get out."

"So you came back to St. Louis?"

"Yes, pregnant with you. Your dad and I had dated in high school, and he'd even asked me to marry him in my senior year. I had been too full of starry visions to imagine just settling down and working while he finished college, so I'd gone off to California."

She leaned slightly across the table, genuine pain on her face. "Your father is a sweet and kind man. I came home pregnant, and he offered to marry me anyway. We eloped a week later. Then you came six months after that."

Justin's eyes widened. "Wait a minute. Then you mean…Dad is not my father?"

She took a napkin from the table to wipe her eyes. Slowly she said, "That's right. Dad is not your biological father. But he *is* your father. He has loved you and raised you as if you were his own. In all this time he's always called you his son—even in private with me. Unfortunately, we haven't been able to have more children. We thought about adopting, but we just never did anything about it when you were younger, and now you're almost fourteen." She looked out through the bay window.

"When were you going to tell me this?"

She looked back. "About dad not being your biological father? We always meant to. It just never seemed to be the right time." She stretched out her hand, but he didn't take it. "I'm so sorry, Justin."

"What—what does dad think about the movies?"

She shook. "He—he doesn't know about them."

"What?"

She looked down at her coffee again. "When I came back broke and pregnant, I was so ashamed. But he told me that he'd marry me and raise the baby as if it were his. He was so good and decent. I just couldn't tell him about those movies, too. I hated them—hated myself. I just told him that I'd gotten pregnant, and he hugged me for a long time and said, 'It's okay.' Justin, I've meant to tell him, but it was never the right time. Can you imagine how I've lived in fear that you or your dad—or a friend or our pastor—would find out? They're so terrible. I've just been praying that no man I know would pick up those movies. I never imagined that you would see me in one at age thirteen."

Justin's voice rose. "So my mom was a porn star and my dad is not my dad. This is certainly a great day! Do you think I should tell Dad—him?"

"I—I wish you wouldn't. I think after all this time that he would forgive me. But I don't want to hurt him."

"Do you want him to find out like I did?"

She wiped her eyes. "No. I've never known what to do. I know that once I became a Christian, I was forgiven. That for eternity I'm clean again. But I also know that there are still consequences in this life. I hope that you can forgive me. I was young and didn't know what I was doing."

Justin lowered his eyes for a moment. "I guess I'm not really mad at you. I'm just so…"

"—Disappointed and embarrassed," his mom said.

"Yes. Disappointed and embarrassed. And scared that others will find out. Including, I guess, Dad."

"If I could take it all back, I would."

He was silent.

"How *did* you and Paul come to see the movie?"

Justin turned red. "Paul found a bunch of movies that his dad had locked in a file cabinet."

"I know Paul's folks split up a year or so ago. It must be tough on him. When we first heard that they were in counseling, we offered to help, but Paul's dad basically told your dad to mind his own business."

"Paul says that his mom used to yell at his dad to stop living in a fantasy world."

She shook her head. "There's just nothing good about pornography."

"Here comes Dad," Justin said, as they heard a car turn into the garage.

"I love you, Justin. Please don't be angry with me. And please don't hurt your dad."

"I won't, Mom. But who knows when someone else will find out?"

****

Late that Wednesday evening Paul's father went to his file cabinet and noticed that the movies were not stacked in the order that he always kept them.

He relocked the drawer and walked upstairs. Seeing the light on under Paul's door, he opened it. The son was surprised to see his father at such a late hour.

"Do you know anything about the file cabinet in my study?"

Paul lowered his eyes for only a moment, but it was enough.

"What have you been doing? Have you been watching those movies?"

"Uh, yeah. I, uh, have watched, like, a few of them."

"Paul, those are *adult* movies, and you're only thirteen."

"Yeah, well. I know. But you know...they're pretty exciting." He tried to smile.

"Did anyone watch them with you?" There was no smile on his dad's face.

"Well, the first time, Justin did."

His father continued to frown.

"Since then I've watched a couple of them by myself. Oh, Dad, you won't believe this. One of the women in 'House Party III' looks just like Justin's mom."

Lie #9: Pornography and promiscuity are victimless crimes.

Truth: Both pornography and promiscuity eventually harm everyone who participates, and their families. The price for just a few minutes of imperfect pleasure is a combination of broken relationships, disease, unwanted pregnancy, or even death.

http://leaderu.com/orgs/probe/docs/pornplag.html
Psalm 101:3
http://www.cwfa.org/articledisplay.asp?id=2041&department=CW
        A&categoryid=pornography
1 Thessalonians 5:22
http://www.beliefnet.com/story/61/story_6116_1.html
http://www.cwfa.org/articles/6262/LEGAL/pornography/

For the latest updates go to www.tenliesandtentruths.com

Notes:

Ten Lies and Ten Truths

10

Two Lists

Late Friday morning Brian Thurman was summarizing that week's lesson, near the mid-point of his ten-week *Time Management and Goal Setting* course. The twenty top executives and managers of Core Systems took extensive notes as Brian wrote each key point on the white board in their corporate training room.

"So after you have set your long-term Dreams and have then derived the specific Goals which fit those Dreams—those that are achievable in six months to five years—the next step is to write an Action Plan for each Goal."

"Then list the hurdles that stand in the way of each step. And finally the solutions to each of those hurdles."

There were smiles and nods around the room as this synthesis of their first lessons came together. Brian continued, "If everyone in the company has agreed to the company's goals, and the Action Plans are combined together from the Mail Clerk to the CEO, the company can accomplish almost anything." He capped the marker and set it in the tray. "In the coming weeks we're going to implement that planning process. Any questions?"

No hands were raised. Brian nodded. "I've enjoyed your input and participation so far, and I look forward to next week's class."

The management team pushed back from their tables, talking, sharing notes, and beginning to shift gears from training to the tasks of the day. The CEO, Ray Walters, ten years younger than Brian, came to the table and extended his hand, beaming. "This is just what we've needed. We have a great team, but we haven't always been pulling in the same direction. Your course is already having an impact on how we approach problems and challenges. Thank you so much."

Brian smiled and returned the handshake. Today's lesson was always a favorite with the companies he advised, when the "light bulb" of recognition went off, and the previous weeks' work finally fit together for a reason.

"Thanks, Ray. You do have a great team. I enjoy teaching them. It will be interesting to see which goals they pick to work on next week."

"Yes, yes it will. Thanks again. We'll see you next week."

Driving back to his office, Brian thought about the ten prospecting calls he would make that afternoon. As part of implementing what he taught, Brian was faithful about making at least thirty new prospecting calls every week. So far he'd only made twenty. Friday afternoon he would settle in with the list of new companies in town and "Dial for Dollars," as they called it around the office. The calls were one of several action steps in fulfilling his own company's income goal for that year.

Brian was coming up on his forty-third birthday. He'd been a Goal Setting/Time Management consultant for fifteen years, ten with his own company. He had helped thousands of people in hundreds of companies attain their goals—or certainly at least get closer to them. It was very satisfying work. He, Marilyn, and their three children planned each month as part of their family's annual plan, and it would soon be time to finalize the year's vacation activities. He couldn't imagine why everyone wouldn't embrace the techniques he taught once they heard them, and it was with that fervor that he always approached his prospecting calls.

Yet...

Occasionally a small voice spoke to him. *This isn't all.* Brian knew the value of faith and tried to practice his Christian principles in his work and his home. In fact, he felt that his entire business was devoted to helping people be better stewards of life's most irreplaceable asset: time. He often wove Christian ethics—without labeling them as such—into the examples he used in his talks. He truly believed that in helping people become more efficient and more successful, he was in a small way helping God build His Kingdom on earth. But the voice would occasionally nag at him—more often in recent months, and it happened again on the short drive that day. What could it mean?

That evening they had dinner with Marilyn's parents, Bill and Joyce Demere. His father-in-law, retired now, had been a small town attorney, forty miles from the larger city in which they all now lived; and his mother-in-law had been a high school teacher. Marilyn had two brothers and two sisters. Her family had never been wealthy, but as far as Brian knew they had never wanted for anything.

What everyone in their family loved most about Bill and Joyce were their stories. Brian often thought that Bill must have known every person in his hometown, and had at least five stories about each one. And Joyce seemed to have followed her students' joys and pains throughout their lives with such tenacity that even now not a week went by that she was not having lunch or a meeting with a former student, his or her spouse, or children.

Their stories had a way to touch the heart, and the kids loved them. There was a richness to his parents-in-laws' lives that Brian assumed was from an earlier time.

That evening, after a good dinner and several great stories, the children had gone on to other things. The adults relaxed at the dinner table with their coffee and dessert.

Brian leaned back in his chair. "Joyce, after hearing how you've continued to help that family for thirty years, I have to ask—how have you kept up with those people all this time?"

Joyce smiled. "Oh, years ago I started to keep the rosters from each of my classes. I'd pray over the children every day, by name. And then I realized that it would be good to have specific things to pray for in each case. So I started asking them what I could pray for. And I'd ask them to be sure to tell me when a prayer was answered so I could cross it off the list. Anyway, I started that with my first tenth grade class…Let's see, it's been almost fifty years ago. Do you believe that, Bill? And I've kept it up ever since."

Her husband nodded at his wife but spoke to Brian. "She's got two big journals. You wouldn't believe 'em. She has *every* student from every year she taught. What she's been praying, how the prayers were answered, new requests, addresses, phone numbers, children. She knows about almost every one of them, and they talk all the time with 'Mrs. Demere.'

"Then when Marilyn and our other kids came, she would always stop whatever she was doing and listen to them. It didn't matter whether the house got cleaned or the laundry done. And listening to them is something Joyce still does pretty regularly."

Marilyn patted her mother's hand. "She always has."

"I think it's sort of like electricity," Joyce smiled. "If I take the time to really connect with someone, then God lets the power flow to change lives, including mine."

"What about you, Bill?" Brian asked. "You seem to know everyone whom you grew up with."

Bill laughed. "And a few more, I guess. I don't have a journal like Joyce does. But I have always tried to be on the lookout for people who need some help—maybe a little money, a nudge finding a job, a little counseling when a marriage hit a rough spot. It's been sort of a habit of mine for a long time. It seems like when you do that, people come back to you. So I've connected and reconnected with people. If you keep your ears open, you learn a lot about people. That usually leads to more ways to help them. Or to suggest how they might help others. Then it just repeats. You know, it's really kind of fun."

Brian considered his father-in-law's words before he spoke. "It's actually been a lot of work, hasn't it?"

The older couple looked at each other. "Work? No, I wouldn't say that," Joyce answered. "Like Bill said, it's really kind of fun. What life is all about."

"But I mean you've thought about it. You've kept some notes. Been intentional."

"Well, I guess if that's work, then Okay, we've worked at it. But the notes have been to jog my memory. The 'work' is just talking to people. Listening, mainly."

✳✳✳✳

The next morning Brian, Marilyn and their children attended Sunday school and church. Their pastor, Ron Taylor, chose to speak on relationships. He cited numerous Bible verses, from Genesis 1-3, Romans 1, 4, 14-16 and 21, and Luke 15, all showing that God had created people in order to have the joy of fellowship with them, not to use them as servants or slaves. Taylor recounted all the times that God *spoke*, indicating His desire for communication, from the creation of the universe to the teachings of Jesus. In fact, the Apostle John referred to Jesus as "the Word."

He explained that Adam ruptured God's expectation of relationship through sin, the exercise of his God-given free will, and that God had finally sent his Son, Jesus, as the once and for all payment for that sin, so that the relationship could be restored, sinner by sinner.

"God doesn't first call us to *do*," Taylor said. "Rather he first calls us to *be*. To be in fellowship with Him. To have a relationship with Him so that we can learn to conform our hearts and minds to His ways. To let Him listen to us. To let the Holy Spirit dwell in us, so that we think His thoughts and speak His words to others, building those further relationships.

"Look how Jesus touched every person he met, from the Samaritan woman to the young ruler. First, he met them where they were, and found out about them, before giving them a Do List. If we think about the people who have influenced us the most, I believe that we are as much influenced by who they *are*, and the genuine concern they have for us, as we are by what they have done. And the only way to express that concern is through a relationship that builds deep and lasting two-way conversation."

When Taylor concluded, Brian knew that this was one of those times when the message seemed to have been written personally for him.

That evening Brian went into his study and spent an hour reading the texts that Ron Taylor had cited, plus some others. And he prayed.

On Monday morning he asked his assistant to reschedule as many of his commitments as possible for the following week. He spent the day reading the Bible, praying, and fasting. That afternoon he made a short list of people with whom he wanted to talk, starting with Ron Taylor, plus others who had been mentors or who had served on his Board of Advisors over the years.

On Tuesday and Wednesday he had six of those meetings and spent more time in prayer. On Wednesday afternoon, he started writing.

****

Friday morning as Ray Walters and the management team at Core Systems gathered in their training room, Brian was in the parking lot praying. Dressed in his usual blue blazer, gray slacks and an open collar shirt, he joined the class just before 8:30. They took their seats. Brian walked to the front and placed some notes on the head table in front of the white board.

The room quieted.

"Thank you for being here for our sixth week. I'm looking forward to hearing the Action Plans that you've written for the company. I'm sure that after a few weeks of refinement we'll finish with five to ten key plans which will move Core Systems to a whole new level of activity and profitability over the next 24 months."

Everyone smiled, and Brian could see a few heads nodding. He took a deep breath. "But we're going to do something different today." Immediate looks of concern. "We've talked for five weeks about being more efficient with time; and we'll cover specific Action Plans—both corporate and personal—in the coming five weeks. But I've decided, if Mr. Walters concurs, to make this a twelve-week course, and I'd like to insert two lessons that I now believe should have started the course."

More looks of concern. Ray Walters turned his head slightly to one side.

Brian took another deep breath. "What we've covered so far has been absolutely accurate and useful. It's just that we've been focusing on *what* to do, and we left off the most important thing, which is *why* to do anything.

"If you're like me, you've probably had some sort of *To Do* List for many years. We're helping improve and focus your List with this course, so that your short-term *Do's* are aligned with your important long term *Do's*.

"But today we're going to start on creating another list, one that is both more challenging and more rewarding to make: It's our *To Be* List. "

Almost everyone in the class looked from side to side.

"I don't know about you, but I've been doing and doing and doing. What I haven't been is being."

Everyone was looking at Brian, waiting.

"Here's my point, and it's a very serious one. We are all doing, and becoming more efficient at it. My concern is that if the *why* we do something isn't related to another person or to other people, then we're just spinning our wheels. Ultimately, we will be shallow, sad and frustrated. I'm admitting to you that I've lost touch with the why—with those *people*. And if you're the same, then it's vitally important that before we do any more doing, we first do some being, some relationship building."

There were a few smiles, but mostly confused faces.

"Who is important to you? Whom have you lost touch with? Who do you want to do something for in your limited future on earth? With whom do you have a strained relationship? Who might give you a different perspective on what's important to do, and wouldn't it be good to have that input *before* you make your *To Do* List? "

There were a couple of nods and some fidgeting. And a few arms folded tightly across chests.

"As a final introduction to this subject, I want to add a personal note. I think this is so important because I believe it is divine." Brian stepped out closer to the class and raised his hands slightly. "I know that we all come from different faith backgrounds, and this is not a course on religion. But I want you to understand me, as the teacher. I don't believe that you can read the basis of my faith—the Bible—without being convinced that relationship and fellowship are at the very core of God's intent for us, first with Him and then with each other. I'll be glad to share references with anyone who is interested after class, but I just want everyone to understand that I feel these next two lessons are actually the reason for the whole course."

The class was silent. Brian smiled. "All right, let's get started."

Using many examples from his own experience, including the preceding week, from literature and the Bible, Brian talked to an attentive audience.

As he neared the end of their time, he said, "And with all of that background on the importance of relationships, you can imagine how difficult it is for me to confess to you that I am a *To Do* Addict. I think many people share my addiction, particularly those of us who consider ourselves to be 'successful.' It can have a power over us that we almost can't explain. There is an initial legitimate truth about it that we then overdo. We have to fight it every day, in order to keep it from becoming our god."

As he looked around the room, he saw only serious faces.

"So here's what I'd like you to do. First, create what I'm calling a *To Be* List. It's simply a list of people, which I'll describe in a minute. The second part of the assignment is to go and spend significant time with the people on your *To Be* List. Since at least some of us are addicts, I want you to invoke the *No Do* Rule. Fight the temptation to *Do* something with them. I want you to stretch muscles that you probably haven't used in a while, especially those two sticking out on either side of your head."

He noticed people looking around the room at each other, some smiling.

"Now divide this list into three groups: Family, Friends, and Business. Add at least five people to each group. You should be able to complete this part of the assignment by tomorrow, which will then give you two weeks to do the main part: Go and *Be* with them.

"Is there someone with whom you should be close but with whom, for some reason, there is an impasse? Start with your spouse and your children, if you feel that *To Do* has gotten in the way of those relationships—and I can tell you in my case it definitely has.

"Ask questions. Find out about *them*, rather than rattling on about yourself. For your Business list, choose a few within Core Systems, but the majority should be outside the firm: customers, suppliers, even competitors. Here you may have to bend the *No Do* Rule and invite them to a ball game, golf outing, or something else, but keep it one-on-one if you possibly can. The idea is to create an environment in which a relationship can blossom through conversation, not an event that can be checked off.

"For a few of you this may all seem crazy—that I'm asking you to do what you've always just done. I salute you, just like I salute those who are already organized when we're focused on the *To Do* List. But I suspect that in this group of managers, the *To Be* List may be the greater challenge.

"All right. Is everyone clear?" No one spoke. "You have my phone number if you need any clarifications or have any questions. Our goal is to return in two weeks with as much Being time as possible, so make your list by tomorrow, and I look forward to hearing your reports. By the way, I'll be doing the same."

****

Three members of the class called over the next two weeks, asking for advice on specific situations. Ray Walters, who had seemed a little nervous, if not unhappy, never called. As the class day drew closer, Brian prayed daily and, as he had promised, worked on his own *To Be* List.

When the two weeks were up, Brian walked into the training room just before 8:30. A quick glance showed him that almost everyone was there, though the room was not as noisy as it had been two weeks before.

As the Core Systems executives took their seats behind their tables, Brian went to the front, took out his notes, and spoke.

"Good morning. I hope you had an eventful two weeks. I'd like to get some feedback."

Several hands went up. He called on a middle-aged man on the right side.

"I haven't talked—really talked—with my younger brother in I couldn't tell you how long. He was first on my *To Be* List. So I called. We agreed to meet at a restaurant we both know, about half way between here and where he lives." He smiled, "We wound up talking for three hours. I found out a lot about my nephew and nieces that I didn't know. My brother has some problems that I think I can help him with. It was great. We're going back in three weeks with our wives. He's first again on next month's *To Be* List, which I've already started."

More hands. Brian nodded to a younger woman in the front row.

"I've had that same situation with my father since I was a teenager. So I called and went over last Saturday. He loves to work in the garden, so we worked together getting it ready for the new season. I feel like I'm reconnected with him for the first time in many, many years. And there are two or three things where each of us is going to give the other a hand. Thank you so much for the *To Be* List."

Ray Walters raised his hand from the middle of the room, and Brian nodded. "Well, I frankly thought that this was sort of a crazy idea when you told us about it two weeks ago. You know, too touchy-feely. A waste of valuable time. But then I figured how much we're paying you for this course, and you added two extra weeks, so I decided I'd try it. I made the list and then I had lunch with two customers and two suppliers. I told them that I didn't want to talk about business, which they couldn't believe, and tried to do anyway, but I wouldn't let'em!" Everyone laughed.

"Once we got past that, we had a great time. We talked about our families, the kids' schools, trips—and, interestingly, after we'd run out of all the standard chitchat, since I wouldn't let them talk about business, we actually got onto some pretty interesting stuff. A previous addiction. Some very talented kids. A marriage in trouble—and I think I know someone who can help. A new home search. A very sick parent. Why haven't we been doing this before?"

"Indeed," Brian agreed, touched by Walters' candor.

Almost everyone in the room shared an experience or two from their *To Be* List that had impacted them in a powerful or unexpected way. Most stories were happy. A few were poignant. Everyone listened.

"I guess I should share as well," Brian said, when the others had all spoken. "I…several years ago a guy I had known and worked with for a couple of years, Don— we—well, we had a falling out. The reason doesn't even matter now. But we had sharp words on two occasions, once in front of others. The last words Don heard from me were in anger. It had sort of bugged me on and off, but never enough to do anything about it.

"Until the *To Be* List. I put him on it. I think I made him number five, hoping I wouldn't have time to get to him." There were smiles. "But it turned out that others didn't answer their phones, so I had to call him. Don was surprised and defensive. He finally agreed to meet. I know that he likes to exercise, so I suggested that we meet at a park near his home one afternoon and walk a few miles."

Brian swallowed hard. "I started by asking his forgiveness for the way I had behaved, and when he saw that I meant it, he forgave me." Brian smiled. "It was like this weight was lifted from me. And I could see that it affected him, too. There's just something about forgiveness that changes all other human equations. That's part of the divine stuff I was talking about. Anyway, I also told him that I now understand his side of the issue and I asked him to start over again with me. He said he would."

Brian looked up and smiled. "We agreed to walk again the following week—I clearly need the exercise—and I told him that I thought I had some leads that could help him in business—Don's very talented."

He paused. "When I arrived at the park last week, he wasn't there. I waited and called his home, but there was no answer. I finally went on, and then an hour later I called again. His wife answered." Brian slowed down and swallowed, "She was frantic and told me that Don had been in a terrible accident that afternoon, and she'd just returned from the hospital, but was going back. The doctors didn't know if he would make it through the night."

Brian took out his handkerchief and wiped his eyes. "Marilyn and I went straight to the hospital. We prayed with his wife and family. Anyway, at about three in the morning the doctor came to get his wife, because they thought the end was near. But we prayed and prayed."

Brian smiled and wiped his eyes again. "I'm happy to say that Don made it through that night, and the next day. But that was a week ago, and they're still not sure if he'll be okay.

"I can't tell you how glad I am to have reconnected with this old friend, and how we're praying for him and his family. I can't imagine how I would have felt if we had not reconciled the week before.

"And if I'd only had a *To Do* List that week, I would have never called him. But I did call him, because I'd written his name on my *To Be* List."

The room was silent for several heartbeats. Finally, Brian said, "I hope you agree with me that the *To Do* List is always important, but that you'll never again start a *To Do* List without also having a *To Be* List already filled in next to it. And that we'll be just as intentional about our relationships as we are about our actions."

There were nods around the room

"So your homework for next week is to take all that you've learned over the last two weeks, and what we've talked about today, and start over on your Plan of Action. I suspect that some of the goals and action steps may be slightly different. If so, I salute you for taking this time to start answering the *Why*, before you get too far into the *What*."

When Brian finished, everyone applauded. He smiled. They stood, but few left the room.

Ray Walters walked forward and shook Brian's hand. "Thank you very much, Brian. You've made an incredible difference to us, as individuals and as a company."

Brian nodded. "Thank you. But I can't take credit for any of this. It all came from God. It's like electricity. If we take the time to really connect with people, then He lets the power flow to change lives."

Walters returned his smile. "You know, I've heard that expression before. Hey, I think I've just connected some dots. I grew up about forty miles from here. Did you have Mrs. Demere, too?"

Two Lists

Lie #10: There will always be more time to start or to mend important relationships. Hard work is more important than relationships.

Truth: None of us knows how much time we or those around us have to be together. Relationships are the key to a rich and fulfilled life. Personal interaction is how we influence others, and how we grow ourselves. If we major on the minors, we will look back on a life that may have accomplishments, but few relationships, family, or friends. Focus on those people who are most dear, and then move out to others before they are gone.

Ecclesiastes 3:1-7, 11
Ephesians 5:15-21

For the latest updates go to www.tenliesandtentruths.com

Notes:

General Resources:

Isaiah 59:14&15   2 Thessalonians 2:9-13
Jeremiah 7:28   John 8:44-46
John 18:37&38   John 8:32
2 Timothy 2:3&4   1 John 4:6
Colossians 2:8   2 Corinthians 10:3-5
2 Timothy 2:24-26
www.frc.org/get.cfm?c=RESEARCH

AFTERWORD

We hope that this book has challenged you to question whether you really know the truth about these ten issues.

And we hope that we have encouraged you to pursue the truth until you are certain.

As many have said, truth is so important because if we cannot invoke truth to settle an argument or to chart a course, then those decisions are made by whomever has the most power. In a society that does not seek, honor and elevate absolute truth, then the strongest bullies are free to make their own rules, and that means that others will suffer. Adhering to the truth, far from putting people in straight jackets, actually gives them the greatest freedom and strength.

The truth will set you free.

If you have not already done so, we invite you to visit www.tenliesandtentruths.com. We will update it regularly with the newest and best resources in all of these areas. Please visit it often. And we particularly ask you to suggest additional resources on each issue. To do so, please send resource information or website addresses to resources@tenliesandtentruths.com.

At last count, over one hundred people participated in helping to write this book, and it is impossible to thank all of them by name. To all who read and said "Keep going, I want this book next week," we can only say thank you.

Several people made specific contributions at crucial points. Susan Yates, Stan Gilespie, Pamela Neu, Bryant Wright, Michael Youssef, Ron Ervin, John Walley, Woody White, Jim Reimann, Sharon Ward, and Chuck and JoElyn Johnston were particularly helpful. Thank you.

We must give special thanks to the AXIS Class at Church of the Apostles in Atlanta. These thirty and forty-somethings bravely served as Beta testers as we refined each story to insure its relevancy in today's world. Thank you.

James Saxon, Stan Carder and Del Tackett were instrumental in providing many of the references. Bob and Shelley Morgan loaned the porch on their Highlands home for inspiration and writing. It was a joy working with our son, Marshall, who focused his gifts on the cover design and graphics details. And Suzan Robertson is an incredibly gifted editor. Of course, any mistakes or oversights are my responsibility alone.

Please keep us in mind and stay in touch as you continue to seek the truth in your own life.

ALSO BY

PARKER HUDSON

On The Edge
ISBN 0-9666614-0-0
Edge Press, LLC

As I read the last chapter of *On The Edge,* I found my heart so full of the Holy Spirit that I thought I would explode. When I closed the book for the last time, I realized that I was crying....I cannot tell you how this book has changed my life and my husband's.

Lori Wells

I finished your book *On The Edge* a few months ago and reflect on its content often. I can honestly say that no novel has ever had as much real and emotional effect on me. I find myself praying more....The final few pages put me in the presence of God...I finished those pages overcome with emotion and sobbing with joy.

Jim Ezell

The President
ISBN 0-9666614-1-9
Edge Press, LLC

I just finished *The President* after being unable to put it down for the past six days. It is a great book!

Phyllis Trail

The President really overwhelmed me. It is possibly the most powerful book I've ever read.

Lee A. Catts

I just finished reading *The President.* Thank you for such a stirring, challenging work. I just wish it were a work of history and not fiction.

Thomas McElroy

Available at www.edgepress.net